Building
A Dynasty!

Rose's Story
Vol III

Carla M. Cuffee

Table of Contents

Prologue

The Dime Divas' careers have taken off in major ways.

Come to find out that Ruby is a Mogul in Lending; She is an Investor.

On the same line as the Shark Tank Moguls, yup, that's what she does and the name of her company Is A Great Mind, **AGM Investments** for short.

Scarlet seems to have been diving more and more in her line of lipware, Scarlet Kisses. Since Rose's birthday party, Scarlet now has ten additional shades of color lipware. Her line of lipware comes in a velvety Matted finish and can be purchased in a high or semi-gloss ware. She's also looking to label the name Scarlet Kisses on fashion designs.

Bubbles no longer wanted to be called Bubbles. Now that she's soon to be turning thirteen years old. She wants everyone to call her by her birth name, Me'chelle.

Rose and Big Eaze have been sailing the Mediterranean Sea for the past six months since their wedding. Not only did Big Eaze purchase Rose a super yacht. He has also purchased them a new home in the Bahamas.

The Event Planning business has been on a fast pace, and Diamond Event Center has been in high demand, Since Rose's birthday party.

Chapter 1

The Dime Diva

Ruby has been running "Diamonds" alone, while Scarlet has been promoting her lipware overseas in Paris.

She has hired a much-needed personal assistant named Bridgett, who has been by her side for almost a year.

Bridgette started immediately working with Ruby on scheduled events. It has been nonstop events for Diamonds and Ruby welcomed the help.

She has not found the time between her busy schedule to hire an assistant for Scarlet. She knows that the business must go on even though her heart and mind are set on traveling the globe, searching for potential clients, wanting to invest in new ideas. She's hoping to find the next great mind.

Her lifelong dream is to invest in her dreams and aspirations in the hope of becoming an inventor. She loves the beginning stages to the results of the invention process.

When meeting new clients, they present new innovated ideas, some are good and possibly on a new path of owning a patent, and then some are bad, resulting in failed attempts. She has also met inventors that have ideas on how to improve existing products.

Besides her family, that's where her heart is.

She employs a team of six considered the research team. Their jobs are to scan the globe in search of the next great mind.

So, Ruby is stretched pretty thin, running two businesses and being a full-time mom, wanting the best for Me'chelle, who now wants to dabble in the world of fashion.

But she only schedules summer travels, for now. It's a long and tedious process, but she's bound in search of the next great mind.

Chapter 2

In Town

Scarlet and her Glam squad are home from Paris. The past six months had been grueling. She is exhausted from attending countless meetings to promote her label.

Scarlet prepares for some much-needed downtime, and while in deep thought, she prepares a bath and takes off her makeup. She turns to look at herself in her custom-made mirror, made to look like Scarlet red lips. *"My brand is rewarding, and I'm making a dent in the lip fashion world. I want all women of ethnicity to pull from my lipware out of their purses. They'll go to work, walk the halls of colleges, they'll be wearing my lipwear in movies, commercials, fashion shows. Scarlet Kisses will have its own label. YES! Watch out for my label."* She smiles at herself.

She walks into her huge bathroom, steps into her oversized sunken tub filled with hot fragrances.

Meditating while admiring the glowing candles around the tub and marble floor, while steam from the hot water rises above the flickering candles, she continues in deep thought while soaking her tired muscles. *What's on the agenda for the next two months?*

Scarlet knows her schedule would need to be clear because Scarlet and her Glams will need to attend the next hottest fashion show to be hosted in London in June.

"Maybe I'll bring Bubbles with me. She's been hitting me up lately, talking fashion, hmm ... I wonder what that's all about."

As she continues to enjoy the sweet aroma and enjoy a little quiet time, her phone rings, she sees that it's Ruby calling.

Scarlet answers the call.

"What's up, Diva?" said Scarlet.

"A whole lot," said Ruby, "how long are you home?"

"Ah, I'm guessing for about two months, unless my Glams find a worthy fashion show to hit up. Why, what's up?"

"Just wanted to know what your plans were, that's all. I already know what you're currently doing, every time you come back from overseas, your routine hot, smelly soaks."

Between laughs, Scarlet said, "You're jealous."

"Yea, Yea, let's meet for breakfast," said Ruby.

"Sounds great. Where and what time?" asked Scarlet.

"Ah, 9:30 a.m., let's meet at 'Happy Hollow,' you do remember that they have the most scrumptious pancakes, right?"
"I'm in the mood for homemade pancakes, and Rose is still out of the country."

"Happy Hollow it is," said Scarlet, "will Bubbles be joining us?"

"Oh, I forgot to tell you," said Ruby. "You know Bubbles will be turning thirteen soon, and she no longer wants to be called Bubbles."

Scarlet's eyebrow raises.

"She wants for us to use her birth name," said Ruby.

Scarlet giggles. "Oh, Bubbles," said Scarlet, "she is growing up! But that's fair. She's no longer an adolescent, but coming into her teens. I'm not sure if you are aware of this, Ruby, but while in Paris, she's been hitting me up about fashion, the runway. Do you know anything about this? It's a hard job, and those girls really don't have much of social life."

"Yea, yea, she may be keeping up with creating her designs. I really don't know; she has so much going on. But if so, I will only allow her to model for catalogs, not the runway. She needs to finish school first."

"Good, but if it's okay with you and seeing how you travel the summers. How about I take her with me and let her see what goes on in the background. You know, let her shadow with one of my Glams," said Scarlet.

"Will talk more about that at a later time," said Ruby.

"Agree," said Scarlet, "so breakfast at 9:30 a.m. I'm on my way to sink in my plush bed that's been calling me every night while in Paris."

The Divas laugh and hang up their lines.

Chapter 3

Breakfast at Happy Hollow

Both Divas were sure happy to see each other; hugs and smiles were shared between the two.

"It seems like forever," said Ruby. "You looking a bit tone. What, you've been in the gym in your spare time!"

"Really," said Scarlet, "like I have spare time even to sit down and have a decent meal. It's been nonstop for me!"

"Well, I like to hear all about it, and then we can compare on who needs time off," laughs Ruby.

They both laugh while walking into the restaurant.

Ruby asks to be seated in a quiet area, seeing how they would need to be discussing Diamonds' business affairs.

The hostess picked up menus for the Divas and led them towards the back area, which they were seated in a window seat.

Happy Hollow was a vibrant place; lots of families came in for their homemade meals. The waiters and hostesses are so charming like they really try to get to know you on a personal level. They like to remember your favorite meals, your favorite beverages even your favorite desserts. They've been seen talking to the guest about sporting events or the latest reality tv shows.

The restaurant sits in a bustling shopping area, where there are more restaurants than you can count with two hands.

But Happy Hallow tops them all. It's surveyed year after year, and the trophies can be seen throughout the restaurant.

Each year the restaurant hosts a summer cook-off, in which they bring in a live carnival concert. All sorts of gaming could be seen throughout the carnival. Of course, the other restaurants down the strip bring their best, always competing. But hands down, Happy Hollow always seems to come out first. It's a family favorite.

Seeing how the Divas came in the early morning, the restaurant employees knew exactly what the Divas came in for, and without even ordering, pancakes arrived in front of them in no time.

Orange juice, coffee and warm syrup for their pancakes were placed on their table, all with a smile from the restaurant Manager.

When the Divas saw it was Natalie, they invited her to sit and chat with them for a moment.

Natalie updated them on what will soon be approaching, the restaurant's annual cook-off and their event planning business.

"Of course," said Ruby, "thanks for asking. Will meet and go over the particulars."

"How about I have Bridgette get back to you with our availability? It shouldn't be later than tomorrow early morning?"

"That sounds great," said Natalie. "I'll be in about 11:00 a.m., have her leave a message regarding the time if I happen not to pick up."

Ruby takes out her phone and opens her task journal. She sets a reminder to have Bridgette contact Natalie at 11 a.m. tomorrow. But she sets the reminder for 3 p.m. today, so she does not forget for tomorrow.

Natalie stands as she appears to leave to get her day started and said to the Divas, "Well, ladies, enjoy your pancakes. They're on the house. It's always a pleasure to see you ladies come into the restaurant."

"Yes ... thank you, you too," said Scarlet.

"Have a great day, Natalie," said Ruby,

The Divas went through their pancakes while talking business.

Ruby wanted to know how they were going to handle Diamonds. She wanted to know how Scarlet would handle her responsibilities at the event center.

"Listen," said Ruby. "I don't want to appear that I'm stepping on your toes, but I also have my company. You remember **AGM** that I continue to run full time. So, we need to somehow agree on how we are to share the responsibilities here at the event center."

"It appears that I'm running the business alone while you're out promoting Scarlet Kisses six months out of the year."

"It's really a lot of work; I've hired Bridgette as my assistance. However, without a staff, I have not given her the green light to become office manager yet."

"We agreed soon, hiring a staff that will be in the position on knowing how we do things at Diamonds."

"But that also will take time, with all the training that comes with it."

Scarlet did not know where to start. She loves what she's doing but also wants to keep the business running.

"Not to sound cruel, but I am here for the next two months. I will work hard, not only on handling my share at Diamonds but also getting assistance," said Scarlet.

"I promise I'll do my part. But I love what I'm doing, and I am going to give it eighty percent of my time."

"Really," said Ruby, "so, you're saying that you're going to give only twenty percent of your time here, that's just not enough," Ruby said, while shaking her head.

"I know, I know, but that's where I'm at right now. It's not going to always be this way," said Scarlet. "Rose has always said follow your dreams, don't give up or give in. I'm just asking for some time, that's all."

Ruby looked into Scarlet eyes and saw her passion in her field of work and felt compassion towards her sister.

With sparks in her voice, Ruby said to Scarlet, "Okay, that's fair, now hire your assistant because we have events lined up and you just witness that we just added another one!"

Chapter 4

Back at The Office

Scarlet plops down and twirls in her chair while attempting to dial an employment agency, Judy Wright Temp Agency. Scarlet knew Judy for some time.

She was also Scarlet's high school Guidance Counselor, and she also runs her family business, which employs temporary to permanent employment. Her Agency specializes in the professional fields of theatre, teaching, landscaping and office professional. She is well sought in part- or full-time employment.

Scarlet thinks, *"I will have my assistant in no time."*

The phone rings … "Hello, Judy Wright Temp Agency. How can I help you?" said Judy.

"Hi, Judy, this is Scarlet Crystal; how are you?"

Judy was surprised to hear from her former student, and you can hear the excitement in her voice as she recognizes Scarlet's voice.

"Hey, Scarlet, how are you?" Judy goes straight into babbling. "I see you tearing up the runway with the new shades of lipware. They are popping hot on the models. I love the new shades, especially how you mix them to give it a dramatic look. I'm like … wow! like a piece of art. I must say, it is awesome seeing you grow into this professional businesswoman, working straight from the capital of the fashion world (Paree)" Judy laughs.

"I guess you can tell that I'm a follower of your social network, but I always believed in you, Scarlet. I knew you were destined for greatness," said Judy. "You were always serious about your future."

"Thanks, Judy and that's correct. I've always been serious about how I was going to shape my future. But I have to admit that I was not thinking of the lip fashion world by far, but now that I'm in it, I'm going full speed. It's all a learning experience for sure, but I'm enjoying every bit of it," said Scarlet.

"I know what you mean, anything that's your brand, it's going to be a lot of work, but at the end of the day, you're working for yourself and you gotta enjoy that ride," laughs Judy.

"Of course," said Scarlet.

"Now that we got that out of the way, how can I assist you," asked Judy.

"Sure, as you know, I'm away more than I am here in the States, while out promoting my lipware brand. So, I need an assistant here at Diamond Event Center."

"I would like to have a few of your candidates come down to be interviewed for a position here in the office, which would also include working outside the office," said Scarlet.

"Okay, sounds great! I'll get on it right away and fax or email over a few names that work in your background. Give me about a day; I think that I can conjure up about five candidates, sounds good," said Judy.

"Yeah, Thank you so much. Here's my email address at Diamonds." And Scarlet recited her address to Judy, sc@diamondseventceneter.org.

"Awesome, again, I will get on this right away," said Judy, "and thank you for thinking of my agency."

"You're welcome," Scarlet said before ending the call.

Scarlet sits back in her chair for a moment and looks around her office. She is very confident that she will have her assistant up and working before the end of the month.

Chapter 5

Bubbles, aka Me'chelle

Me'chelle, all of twelve and a half years old, already has an eye for fashion. When not busy with school and friends, she sits at her huge drawing table, that's filled with her hand sketch designs. She has blouses in every color, from dresses to T-shirts and skirts in all shapes and sizes (minis, wraps, flare to pleaded, she's also added a skate skirt for the young and hip crowd). She sits there for hours on end, creating new designs.

She holds up a T-shirt, which reads, "I LOVE MY SWAG."
And she does have that swag!

She sits back in her lounge chair, with her wireless headsets in her ear and her hands wrapped in the back of her head, all while thinking that it would be way cool to label her designs as *Scarlet Kisses." I have to get Aunt Scarlet's attention,* thought Me'chelle.

Ruby walks into Me'chelle's room, which Me'chelle hadn't notice right way. She hadn't seen that her mom was standing beside her, looking over all the designs on the table, some under color pencils, and many more under paperweights.

"Wow," said Ruby with excitement in her voice, "there are so many designs, I didn't know that you were still creating them?" Ruby picks up one of Me'chelle's designs and said, "This is really nice and the color, is so vibrant."

Me'chelle now looked up and saw that her mom was looking over her designs. She pulls out her headsets and said, "I've been creating them a little while before I made G'Ma and our wedding attire. That's why I've wanted to see Aunt Scarlet, to get her views on them and the weird thing is that I can be anywhere, and a design comes to mind. I'm flooded with so many ideas. Sometimes it's exhausting, but I love creating them," said Me'chelle.

"Well, my view is that you're good at this," said Ruby.

"Thanks, Mom, you're just saying that because you're my mom," said Me'chelle.

"No, I'm serious, you keep this up and you are going to be amongst one of the youngest designers," said Ruby.

"I would love that; I believe that I am ready to create them live. But from the look of things (Me'chelle pointed at all her designs) I have so many, that I'm gonna need some help," said Me'chelle.

"First things first," said Ruby, "let's get Aunt Scarlet to look them over and then we can go from there."

"Fair," said Me'chelle, "where is she now? I know she's home from Paris. I heard you two had breakfast this morning."

Ruby looks at Me'chelle and said, "I'll give her a call."

Chapter 6

Well, Hello

Scarlet went running to Ruby's home, not only with exciting news on soon to be hiring a personal assistant but wanting to see all the designs created by her very own niece Me'chelle, aka Bubbles.

Scarlet lets herself in at Ruby's home, with her key code that Ruby has for each member of the family. Another of Ruby's investment deals, through **AGM.**

Ruby met with a group of inspiring young ladies, who came up with the idea of key coding residential front home entrance doors. She immediately invested in them. The company started small, but after Ruby had gotten involved and stepped up their marketing, advertising and networking throughout the United States, they now build capital and have several sites across the US. The group continues to stay close in contact with Ruby. They have built a close network of friends.

Scarlet searches for Ruby and Bubbles and finds them both in Me'chelle's room, sitting on the floor, organizing sketches.

"Well, hello," said Scarlet, "let's see whatcha working with." As she pops her shoulders back and forth.

One by one, Me'chelle showed Scarlet her created designs, feeling proud of her work, she sits in anticipation while Scarlet looks over what was given to her. One design that caught Scarlet's attention was a T-shirt branding Diamonds the event center, in sky blue and the name Diamonds had diamonds bursting out all around its name. Scarlet was impressed.

"Hey, missy, you got some skills, is this why you kept hitting me up. All the while I'm thinking you missing your Aunty?"

"Well, I do, but yea ... I'm flooded with so many ideas and thought, who better to look over my designs. I want to create them live, Aunty. I'm amazed as well, and you work up close with models and the runway, you have an open door onto the fashion scene. I'm so excited."

Scarlet laughs and said, "You should be, these are great. Well, seeing how you like to design, do you know how to sew yet? I remember hearing that Carlotta wanted to teach you."

"Awe, no, I don't, but Carlotta has created sketches. There is such a thing as "designers" that just design pieces, right?" asked Me'chelle.

"Absolutely," said Scarlet, "but I would suggest that you take a class in sewing, which I'm not sure about Carlotta's schedule. She's been in Spain for some time now, no telling when she's coming back to the States."

"Either way, let me get in contact with some friends (again her network of friends), and we'll go from there, sounds like a plan," asked Scarlet.

"You bet," said Me'chelle.

Ruby sat on the sideline, letting Me'chelle conduct herself as an upcoming entrepreneur. She thinks to herself, *"I may just be looking at the next **AGM**."*

Scarlet now turns her attention to Ruby. "I also have some good news; I am in the process of interviewing, hopefully, my new assistant."

Ruby, now looking very surprised at Scarlet's comment said, "New, you don't have an old one."

"Very funny, Diva, but yea, I spoke with Judy at Judy Wright Temp agency, and she has set up five potential candidates."

"So, I will be out of the office most of the day tomorrow interviewing. I have set up a meeting station at the Mall on fifth," said Scarlet.

"Good to hear," says Ruby, "because we have an upcoming meeting with a new Client, to meet at Vested on this Wednesday early evening. They've briefly mentioned that they would like to have a dinner party and they're thinking about having about thirty guests to come in on a Thursday evening."

"I'm guessing within a couple of weeks, not sure on the date yet. But it's a fundraiser, they're raising money to open a youth center, and my thoughts are, we're not going to have much time to plan this event. This event will be one of those fast on your feet planning. So, all the help we get will be needed."

Scarlet said, "After my interviews, I will get in contact with a designer."

"Great," Me'chelle agrees with her Aunt Scarlet, and they both fist pump each other in agreement. Me'chelle was very excited. She's ready to put her designs on real cloth in real color and on a real person.

Chapter 7

Interviewing

Scarlet meets with each candidate for about forty-five minutes. She runs down a list of interviewing questions for each candidate to answer.

1. Describe yourself. What are your interests? What are your goals? What makes you, you and describe where you see yourself in five years while working as an event coordinator?

2. Are you able to handle five scheduled meetings a day?

Scarlet stops herself and said, "I'll change that question, possibly eight meetings a day?"

Scarlet understands days working as a coordinator can be challenging. So, she wanted a more in-depth answer.

3. Explain how you would handle it if a client **(1)** called and could not make the meeting at the scheduled time but wanted

to change the time to the **(3rd)** scheduled meeting. But the **(3rd)** scheduled meeting was a high-profile client?
How would you prioritize your day?

4. Sometimes, you would independently work outside of the office, you will need reliable transportation, would this be an issue?

5. On a scheduled event, the weather changes from sunny skies to an overcast cloudy day. The weather changes for the worst a few hours before the event were to take place and your event is an outdoor event. How would you handle that situation? Having a plan (B), what would your plan (B) be if plan (A) falls short?

6. Innovation is key to the event portfolio. Would you say you have that skill in coming up with fresh ideas, thinking outside of traditional lines of business? If so, give me one example that your innovative skills came into play.

Scarlet thanks each candidate while seeing them out of the office. When going back into the rented office space, she falls back in the oversized chair and whispers, "Whew that was a lot." She closes her eyes for what seemed to be a cool ten to fifteen minutes.

She opens her eyes, stands up, smooths out her clothes, picks up her briefcase and walks through the office to meet with the office manager Ted and thanks him for the rented space.

She heads out of the mall towards her truck, gets in and places the briefcase on the passenger seat, drives off heading to Diamond Event Center, but all the while wanting to go home and soak and have a nice quiet dinner.

But she knows that she's on another mission, trying to contact her designer friend in Paris, Bernadette Sequel, to talk with her about Me'chelle Designs. While driving she speaks into her phone to Siri's and requests Siri to call La'Fea Agency in Paris.

The phone rings and kept ringing at least ten times before Bernadette's assistant Charlie, picks up the line and then said to Scarlet that Bernadette is currently with a client and that she would need to leave her a message.

Charlie asks Scarlet, "What time of the day would be the best to reach you?"

Scarlet, not wanting to show she was a little annoyed with Bernadette's new assistance. Before speaking, Scarlet thought, *she must be Bernadette's new assistance, boy did she go through them. Does she not know that I, Scarlet Crystal am in one-to-one contact with Bernadette?*

But not to show that she was annoyed, Scarlet tells Charlie the best time to reach her would be 9 a.m. Eastern time. Scarlet emphasizes Eastern time … that would be 3 p.m. Paris time.

She thanks her for her time, and they both hang up.

Chapter 8

Back in The States

Close to an 11-hour flight, Rose and Big Eaze land on American soil, their car is there to pick them up after retrieving all their luggage.

Travelers were looking in their direction as if they were celebrities. It wouldn't be a surprise, between them both, they had about four to five luggage pieces.

When exiting at baggage claim, the sliding doors open, the cold air hits Rose's face for a moment, and she shivers in the cold. It is an unusually cold crisp day.

"Oh, my goodness," shrieks Rose. "This is unusually cold weather here."

Chase. Rose and Big Eaze's driver was parked right in front of the exit door. He had the limo door open, which they both quickly stepped in while their driver and the airport attendants loaded their luggage into a small minivan that was sent from Big E's Enterprise.

You didn't think that all their luggage would fit in a limo?

They were whisked away in minutes of landing, relieved from their long flight. Rose kicks off her red bottom sling-back sandals and plops her feet on top of Big Eaze's lap while twirling her toes.

With a smirk on his face, Big Eaze got the message and massages Rose feet.

"What," said Rose, "my feet don't stank."

"Well, they don't smell like roses either," said Big Eaze and laughs.

"Okay," said Rose, "whatever!" While closing her eyes and enjoying her foot massage.

From their local airport, it takes a clear thirty minutes to arrive at the Crystal Manor. Chase, their driver spoke into the intercom and asked if there would be any stops before arriving at the mansion. He got no answer from neither.

When rolling down the window, to his surprise, Rose and Big Eaze were fast asleep. He rolls the window back up, all while thinking **they just got in**. He then heads to the Crystal Manor.

The limo finally comes to a gentle stop, he gets out of the limo and taps on the window. Suddenly, Big Eaze scrambles to get his bearings. "What, what, what's going on?" While wiping his face with his large hands Big Eaze said, "I never fall asleep on a road trip."

Rose awakes and stretches and laughs at Big Eaze. "You could've fooled me. I see you asleep often on long road trips. You're just tired from all the partying on the open sea, you'll be ok."

As Rose comes out of the limo, she thanks Chase for the peaceful ride. "I loved the relaxing music; you see that it put us fast to sleep," said Rose.

"Not a problem Ms. Rose, it's a pleasure to be your driver, I'm glad your home," said Chase.

"Well, thank you," said Rose

Evelyn and the staff could see that the limo was coming up the wrap-around driveway and goes to greet Rose and Big Eaze at the massive fountain, which is a place in front of the Crystal Manor.

"Well, hello strangers welcome back to the states we are so glad that you've both made it back safely."

After hugs were exchanged from both women Evelyn said, "What can we get for you both?" While walking back into the mansion.

Rose and Big Eaze enter the mansion.

Rose mentioned that she would love to get into a hot running bath water, filled with rose milk.

"I just want to soak off all the sea salt from the Mediterranean Sea and sit by a fire with a nice glass of red wine, listen to some smooth jazz. Rose shook her head in agreement with her statement ... "Yea that would be all I need for the moment."

Evelyn now turns to Big Eaze and gestures, "You Frank?"

"Awe … I would love to have something to eat, thank you," said Big Eaze while walking up the massive spiral staircase adorned in white and gray marble and railings made of black iron, which runs to the top staircase.

Before Rose was to take her bath, she calls her daughters. With so much excitement in her voice, she Facetimes each.

She Facetimes Scarlet first and Scarlet also being so happy to see her mom back home and said, "I'm coming over right now."

"No." Stopping Scarlet in her tracks, while Rose laughs at Scarlet's remarks, she said. "I need rest, I will call you tomorrow and we'll have a feast on Sunday."

"Well, alright, how long are you here?" asked Scarlet.

"No, the question would be, how long are you here Ms. Scarlet Pooh?"

"Never mind me we'll talk tomorrow, I'm glad your home mom," said Scarlet.

"Thanks, sunshine," said Rose.

Rose now Facetimed Ruby and Bubbles and yells, "Hiiii!" Ruby chuckles, "Well, hello, are you home?"

Me'chelle sitting on an oversize chair in their family room, that's filled with fluffy pillows and yells out, "Hi G'Ma welcome back home."

"Hi beautiful, and yes, we finally got in about two hours ago," said Rose.

"Awesome, we have so much to catch up on," said Ruby.

" Yea that's right, so do I," yells Me'chelle.

"I want to tell you all about my designs."

Ruby smiles at Me'chelle and said to her mom, "I know you wanna rest, so we will see you tomorrow afternoon. Sound good?"

"Of course, and we'll have a feast on Sunday," said Rose.

"That's wonderful, we were starting to miss the family dinners," said Ruby.

Rose laughs and said, "Good night my sweet ♥'s."

Chapter 9

A Sunday Feast

Crystal Manor was full again, when invited to dine at the Crystal Manor, it is in your best interest to show up.

Rose asks all that are invited to dinner, not to come to the dinners in their fancy attire but to come comfortable, *come to eat and have fellowship with one another in a relaxing environmen*t.

Even though the formal dining room, housed a massive dining table, which was top with bouquets of white roses, having a sweet citric aroma, which filled the air. The tall back ivory color seating chairs adorn the same fabric as the ivory color window draperies, which were held open with gold rose embodied clips. The flooring is adorned in gray slated marble.

All seem interested in hearing about the new mansion that Big Eaze had purchased for them in the Bahamas.

From the time of the purchase, anxieties have been running high at Crystal Manor. Rose has been hearing rumors amongst the staff, *will they be selling Crystal Manor, would we continue to have a job, would we be offered a job in Bahamas.*

Rose plans to put a stop to the rumors; she plans to set up a staff meeting come Monday morning.

She wants to sure her staff, that they have a place at Crystal Manor.

This is my home, and I will not be selling my home; this home will stay in my family thought Rose *and what made them even come up with this crazy idea, this is our third home, they haven't been replaced then, where is all this all coming from. Who would even plant that idea in their minds?* Now shaking her head in disbelief. *But for now, we'll eat and be merry.*

At dinner, everyone wanted to hear about their yachting experience. Rose had in mind setting up the projector in the garden, which will show a short video of them on the open sea and their docking experiences, in which they had visited cities down the Mediterranean Sea to experience other cultures.

Rose and Big Eaze were seen out shopping in the native culture districts. They strolled into an evening festival, dancing to the song Havana, they could be seen at a carnival, riding on a Ferris wheel that lit up the night sky.

Rose, soaking up some sun on the beach, while Big Eaze swam in the ocean.

Rose was even seen, braiding the native girls' hair in two French braids. She wanted to show them she had the skills to do hair.

They were seen stretched out on the grass at an outside theatre, which appeared to show a comedy movie on the huge screen. Their faces said it all, filled with laughter while sipping on exotic drinks.

"We had a blast," said Rose, "but I have to admit, there were some rough nights at sea. It wasn't always smooth sailing; I was getting home sick."

"I'm guessing that to be expected Rose, we were out there for six months," said Big Eaze.

The night ended in laughter and many more questions for Rose and Big Eaze to answer.

Chapter 10

Meeting in The Media Room

Rose calls for a staff luncheon, to be held at 1 p.m. in the media room, which was completed in theatre seats. Scarlet had the seats covered in the color of black onyx. The smell of the room was of rich leather.

Scarlet believes it was a well-thought-out and perfect design, a birthday gift for her mom. That room was well over ten thousand dollars, and it was hardly used. The room could hold a party of thirty guests. The screen is over 150 inches in size. When hosting movies, the theatre comes with a popcorn machine a fountain drink machine and candies. It was like going to a movie theater.

The staff was to have lunch and a movie. They were served sandwich rings and chips and dips and pasta salads. No popcorn was served anytime during the movie; they were scheduled to watch a comedy.

Rose wanted the staff to be comfortable and relaxed and not at all tense, but ready to talk after the movie.

The movie ended on a high note with laughter filling the theatre. Once the movie was done, showing the credits, the lights got brighter in the theatre room. Rose being Rose, addresses the staff, she wants to address their concerns regarding the new home in the Bahamas. After a small speech on the purchase of the new home, she opens the floor for discussion.

She said, "I've been hearing rumors about people being let go because we have a new home? I would like each one of you to speak to me with your concerns, regarding the new home in the Cayman Island."

Each addresses Rose with concerns about their future at the Manor.

Rose listens to each one that got up to address their concerns. She then asks the staff, "Have I ever made you feel like this was coming to an end? I mean I have high regards for you here at Crystal Manor. You have been with me for years, you have gone on trips with my family and I, I've treated you as a family member. Frank and I have been gone for six months, for one, we really needed time to get away and yes while yachting and purchasing a new home, we have acquired other businesses. But we are not and let me stress it again. We will not be selling the Crystal Manor. I'm asking you all, going forward to stop with the rumors. If you have concerns, come see me or see Evelyn, she manages your areas. If you are doing your job, you shouldn't have to worry about your job. I'll say this though, we may not be staff every day, but you are salary employees."

"If anyone of you would like other positions within Big E's Enterprises, well, let's talk about it. I don't want you to feel stagnant, I want you to fulfill your dreams, whether it be in hospitality or other areas in the company. There is room for advancement here and I would hope that you feel comfortable enough to talk about it and seek open positions."

One employee had mentioned that they did not have a career path at Crystal Manor and didn't think that there would be.

"We are here in the Mansion and there are employees in Big E's Enterprise, we never thought that we would be able to cross over."

"Are you serious," said Rose. "If my girls thought that way, they would still be working for me, better yet, they run their own companies, outside of the event planning business."

Rose listens to more of her employees talk about advancement within the enterprise. Some were ok where they were but wanting to continue having a job.

Rose thinks while listening to her employees.

I'm coming to see this could be my fault, I have not addressed this as being one company, but how could I. I don't think we officially added Diamonds under Big E's Enterprise. We have not had a formal companywide meeting to announce that we are all under one company and that is Big E's Enterprises.

Rose snaps out of her daydream and said to all fifteen of her staff employees.

"Come the next few weeks, we can schedule meetings on an individual level and see how we can work together and see what fits you, does this sound fair? asks Rose.

They all agreed, and they thank her for the movie and taking the time out to address a sensitive situation.

After the staff left out the media room, Rose asks Evelyn to set up a meeting with Frank.

They would discuss Big E's Enterprise as a whole company.

Chapter 11

Event Planning at Vested

Vested is a fairly new restaurant on Ninth Street and Ruby is not only friends with the owner, but they are also business partners (one more for her portfolio). She has hosted many investment dinners at Vested.

The food is outstanding, it's so popular with the locals, they have now expanded via social media, which helps a great deal in bringing in more outside business.

Lloyd has mentioned to Ruby he has been thinking about opening a small diner that serves breakfast all day.

Ruby in her zone as an Investor asks Lloyd to be sure about the area at which he wants to open the diner.

She said, "The hours of operation (open and close), the food selections and pricing are very important for the area that you plan to bring in a business."

"I suggest that you find a location that allows the patrons easy access via the diner and parking ... that's a plus," said Ruby.

But tonight, she's on another mission, to meet new clients. Young entrepreneurs want to give back to their community.

Ruby and Scarlet arrived at the restaurant, thirty minutes early, going over ideas they would like to present to the clients, while finger foods were being placed on a separate table, that they'd plan on serving to their clients, soon to be arriving.

A team of twelve came into the restaurant at their appointed time and was led to the Divas area. All shook hands and each introduces themselves.

Ruby said to the team of twelve to help themselves to some refreshments before the meeting was to begin.

Right away the Divas were given a copy of the floor plans of the renovated property.

The Divas notice a section of empty blocks on their copy, looking at each other for an answer, they were unsure why that was.

The guest took their seats, while the Divas continue to view the copy of the renovated project.

There was chatter from the group while getting comfortable in their seats.

Scarlet took the liberty to speak to the team of twelve first, which she had a host of questions.

While holding the copy of the renovated project in the air, Scarlet asked her questions.

"From what we were just given to view, I notice several empty blocks. So, I have a few questions."

Would there be a theme to this event, seeing how it is investing in the future of our youths, what ideas are going to be presented at the dinner? Would we need to have pamphlets made up? Possibly a short video or a slide show, to be presented at the dinner?

Scarlet wanted to show Ruby, that she as much as Ruby wants to keep the business running.

"Good you ask, we do have some things in mind," said Gerald, and he pulls out of his briefcase, a small projector.

"I have a slide show, showing the building that we have in mind. Excuse me, the building that we are buying," Gerald corrected himself.

Ruby was excited to be a part of this as well; she was a silent investor in this project. So, she was excited to see firsthand what they would be presenting.

The slide show showed that they were to renovate a dilapidated one-story home, which had about six rooms, a living room a dining room along with a kitchen and two bathrooms, they planned on taking out the old tubs to make as half baths for extra square footage.

Scarlet jumps in and said, "Would you be selling the tubs, which can bring in some revenue?"

You're on to something … thank you for that idea, I don't think we thought about that, matter of fact we have not thought about salvaging anything that could be of good use," said Gerald.

Ruby noticed that one of the twelve was taking notes, possibly filling in the empty blocks.

The home really needed some work, from new, wood floors, to new windows, a fresh new coat of paint, which would be inside and out. The outside front fencing needed repairing, maybe rip out to add new fencing, around the entire property.

The front and back porch would also need to be ripped out and rebuild. The plan showed that they were going to construct a wraparound porch and the outside grounds, just needing some new grass.

The slide show took about fifteen minutes, with Gerald going over the blueprint of the project, overall, it was a great starter.

The Divas thank them for showing what's to come of a great start to the community.

After the slide show...

Ruby stands in front of the group and addresses the group of twelve, "We would like to suggest, the dinner party to be hosted here at Vested."

"Vested is a new restaurant, its vibrant and having an inviting atmosphere will set the right mood and let me not forget to mention, that they have great food," which she hands each one a menu. We can also have the menu tailor to a specific menu if you like."

Ruby said, "I'm sure this is for you and the team to decide, how will you be receiving the funds for this project. Scarlet has some great ideas. But I also like to suggest this really could be a big hit, we can set up a silent auction, possibly of some sort of art or sports memorabilia."

"We could bring in a local celebrity to sing at the dinner. This could also hit your target with all proceeds going towards the project."

One of the twelve said, "Going back to the auction, that's sound like a really good idea, we may just get enough money for after school supplies for several years, if we invest wisely."

"Correct," said Ruby.

"As Scarlet previously mentioned, we can create pamphlets, placing them on tables describing the project... give an outlook on what's to come in the community."

"If we're going with the idea of a pamphlet, would you like a specific theme possibly wording, or a picture of an after-school center or building?"

Gerald who seems to be the speaker for the team of twelve, said they have a team who will be contacting the investors.

"We have several suggestions on presenting the fundraiser to our investors, and we pretty much feel solid with that part of the project."

"But all that you have suggested also sounds great, if you can list these ideas on paper and pass them by my office in a couple of days, he gave both Divas his business card, which would be awesome. I'll share with the entire staff, and we'll get back to you as to what we have narrowed down."

"Okay, we can do that," said Scarlet, as she jotted down the details.

"What day are we planning for the dinner party," asked Ruby, which she was hoping sooner than later, they have a big event coming up soon, which will take more time planning.

"We are thinking within the next four weeks, Gerald looking at the team of twelve for an agreement. "Hoping we'll have all the funds to tackle the first big project (demolition and clean up) and if there's a need for more funds, we then can entertain that idea of an auction," said Gerald.

"Great," thought Ruby, "this is the smallest event for the mon*th.*"

"Must I suggest, if you're thinking on entertaining the auction, get on it right away. You would need to secure a nice piece of art to present to your guest," said Ruby.

Gerald stands and said, "We thank you, ladies, for those great ideas and I believe we all agree to host the event here at Vested."

If we tailor the menu for this event, we'll let you know within a few days. We would then like to add copies of the menu into the invites so that the investors are aware of what would be served at the fund raiser, that evening."

As the team gathers their things to leave. Gerald looks at the Divas and said, "We look forward to a great event within a couple of weeks. We will get everything finalized within a week, so we will be in touch with you by the end of next week. Until then ladies have a great evening and thank you again."

Ruby and Scarlet now standing, both Divas thanking the team.

"Thank you for your business and you all have a great evening as well," said Ruby and Scarlet shaking their guests' hands, while they all were leaving out from their designated dining area.

Scarlet walks back to Ruby and both stayed a little while longer, going over the details of the event.

"Well, for starters I do know that Vested will be open to this event and we'll need DJ. Spinn … if he's free or any other of his DJ's," Ruby said but speaking much quicker.

"We'll need the projector setup in the back, once we are aware of how many we'll be attending the event. I think it's best to have eight to a table and I'll have Lloyd make available, round tables to prevent overcrowding," she said.

"Wow," said Scarlet. "I see you're in your Investing zone." While smiling at Ruby.

"This is a good investment, investing in our youths."

You better believe it, thought Ruby, all while smiling to herself.

After overhearing the staff talking about a center being built at Rose's fiftieth birthday party, it had struck a chord in Ruby's heart, which she stands behind this cause, *investing in our youth's future and with a program, such as this, it will open doors, giving them opportunities, to build life-changing skills and to live out their dream(s) of becoming whatever their heart desire.*

Ruby looks up at Scarlet and said, "Yes indeed, investing in our youth and our community, is a need."

"They are our future *CEO' CFO, our bankers, our realtors, our teachers our presidents.* Every child needing a chance to believe in themselves, yes this is a great cause," said Ruby.

Ruby was a proud silent donor!

Chapter 12

Scarlet Assistant

Most of the day, Scarlet goes over the interviewer resumes and questionnaires and finally wanting to meet a candidate again, not for a second interview, but she wanted Mindy to be her assistant.

So, she calls Mindy and invites her to the office of Diamonds, she wanted her to meet with Ruby and Bridgette and give her a tour of the event center.

Scarlets retrieves Mindy's contact number and preceded to call her.

While Mindy was in the process of making her a cup of tea, she hears her phone ring, she goes to retrieve her phone off her kitchen table, she says, "Hello?"

"Hi, Mindy, this is Scarlet Crystal from Diamond Event Center, how are you on this lovely day?"

"Hi Scarlet," said Mindy sounding very excited to hear back from Scarlet. "I am doing great and you?"

"I'm great, can't complain about this great weather we're having," said Scarlet.

"I'm calling because I would like to set up a second meeting with you to go over more details of the open position. What day would be good for you to come into my office?" asked Scarlet.

"I'm pretty flexible… awe if you give me a day and time, I'll make sure that my schedule is clear," said Mindy.

"Ok great, how about Wednesday about 10 a.m.?" asked Scarlet.

"That sounds good, I will be there," said Mindy.

"We're located on Ten Foxwood Lane, you won't miss us, it's the only white one-story building on the block and we do have onsite parking, which is located on the side of the building," said Scarlet.

"Just to let you know, you may need to block off about two hours of your time, hope this is ok with you?"

"Not a problem," said Mindy. "Thanks for getting back to me and I'll see you at 10 a.m. on Wednesday."

"Wonderful, have a great day," said Scarlet.

"And you have the same," said, Mindy.
Later that day

Bridgette walks into Ruby's office and said she had contacted Natalie at Happy Hollow with their availability. Natalie had agreed to meet with them, that upcoming Monday at 2 p.m., she had also mentioned "If we were available on the Saturday before that Monday, which will work as well."

"Yea that works for me, I'll give her a call back, you'd planned this Saturday off, right?" asked Ruby.

"Yes, I do, I have a prior engagement. You think you'll be able to handle this without me?" asked Bridgette.

Ruby gives Bridgette the side eye. "Huh I know you're kidding." As she laughs out loud.

"Of course," laughs Bridgette. "I know you can handle it and besides Scarlet will be with you. Please take notes as if I was there, I have to know what I am getting involved in."

Ruby laughs again. "Ok, taking notes and checking things off... like a Boss."

Ruby got along well with Bridgette and was very pleased with all that she helps with. She comes in early and is sometimes the last to leave the event center. Ruby likes that she follows up well and has the next day's agenda ready for when they walk in the next morning. She could train staff on how to organize and prioritize their day. Ruby thinks out loud, "She's diffidently a keeper!"

"What's that," asked Bridgette!

"Oh, nothing just thinking out loud," said Ruby.

… when entering the event center. The front doorbell jingles, which rings throughout the event center, informing the staff that someone has entered the building. Scarlet came in walking toward her office and yells out "hello" before going into her office. She has not gotten a call yet from Bernadette in Paris.

It was too early in the morning to be calling Paris, but she did check her voicemail to discover there was a local fashion show that had invited her and three other quests to come and check out the show.

"Thank you, I sure will." And yells out to Ruby they were invited to a local fashion show.

Ruby walks into her office to ask, "What was that?"

"We're invited to a fashion show, here in town, this Sunday at 4 p.m. and I can bring three other guests. It looks like DJ. Spinn will be there. They're also serving food; you think that you would be interested in going?" asked Scarlet.

"Yea, I'm for it, food involved, yup, who else will you be inviting," asked Ruby.

"Rose and Me'chelle of course," said Scarlet.

"Are you sure, Rose doesn't have a dinner party planned, she normally has dinner parties on Sundays. You need to call her and find out," said Ruby. "Also, we have a meeting on Saturday with Happy Hollow."

Scarlet calls Rose and asks what her plans were for Sunday.

"I am resting all day, in my PJ's. I plan on watching TV all day. I have no plans and I do not want any," said Rose.

"Ok, I hear you loud and clear," said Scarlet.

So, she calls some of her friends after her call with Rose with an open invitation.

Chapter 13

Paris Calling

Finally, Scarlet receives a call from Paris, while she was on the phone trying to reach one of her Glams. *Everyone seems lost, No one is answering my calls* thought Scarlet.

She hangs the lineup and answers the Paris's line, before she'd missed the call.

Already knowing the international number but keeping it professional, she answers.

"Hello, Diamond Event Center. How may I help you?"

"Hello, darling," said Bernadette (in a heavy French accent voice), I hear you have tried to reach me a few days ago. What's going on, I thought you would be more than happy to be out of the State, away from this crazy place," laughs Bernadette.

Scarlet laughs out loud, "No way that's my second home. But I had to leave, I still have to run the event planning business with Ruby."

"Of course, darling how is Ruby? We may have some business here in Paris for her," says, Bernadette.

"She's well, I called because you do remember Ruby's daughter, my niece, Me'chelle?"

"Yes, that beautiful sweetheart of a child, if I can remember correctly, we called her Bubbles right," asked Bernadette.

"Yea your right but she's growing up into this beautiful young lady and she has been gifted with design making!"

"She showed me some of her drawings and has mentioned that she is ready to put them on fabric." say's Scarlet, "and they're pretty good."

"I wanted you to see some of her designs or direct me to someone that you suggest that would work well with teen designers."

"Wow!" said Bernadette (you could hear the excitement in her voice). "The whole family is gifted. But my concerns would be Rose, doesn't she have Carlotta to help in design making. I don't want to step on anyone's toes. But for you, my darling. I would love to see her designs, are you coming to the States, or would this be by video call?"

"Well, I have some things up here to take care of first, but I will be there for the Summer fashion show in London," said Scarlet. "So, yes, this will have to be a video call. I do plan to bring her back (Bubbles) with me for the full summer."

"Yes, darling I remember her mother tours the country, investing in potentials inventors, again, we are looking for some known investors in Paris," said Bernadette.

"Great, I'm sure she would be pleased to hear that," said Scarlet.

"When would be a great time to call in for a video chat?" asked Scarlet.

"You know I don't know my schedule, hold the line darling while I get my availability from Charlie. Did you get to meet her, darling, she is fast on her feet. I think she's a keeping this time around."

"Yeah, I did she was unaware of who I am."

"Well, we will get that fixed right away," said Bernadette, before putting Scarlet on hold, what seemed to lag for over ten minutes.

"Sorry Darling, I didn't mean to put you on hold for so long but thank you for your patience. You of all people, know that this place is busy all the time."

"Awe." Bernadette went through her calendar.

"I have a thirty-minute open window next Wednesday evening at 8 p.m., will this work for you?" asked Bernadette.

"We'll make it work," said Scarlet. "Thank you for taking time out to make this call Bernadette, I'm sure Me'chelle is going to be ecstatic to hear, that I finally reach you."

"Yes, Scarlet darling we miss you and your Glams vibes in Paris, it's so empty without you here. Take care of yourself and tell Rose I miss her as well and hope she can make it here soon."

"You bet," said Scarlet, "bye for now."

"Toddles," said Bernadette.

Chapter 14

World Famous Summer Cook-Off

Scarlet and Ruby met up with Natalie at Happy Hollow, early Saturday afternoon. They were to plan the restaurant's annual summer cook-off.

Natalie said they would do something a little different this year and have food booths made up of different food ethnicity and that the owners of Happy Hollow would send a Chef from each of their restaurants.

The owners were so impressed with the success of the cook-offs each year, that they would like to incorporate the idea in other states that have their names.

Natalie said, "We're bringing in about six chefs and we would like for you to help set up."

"Oh, that can be done," said Ruby, "give us the names of the groups that will be participating."

Natalie said, "We'll have South African, West Indies, Bohemian, Brazilian, Irish and of course, American cuisines. We're hoping that this will be a big success this year."

"Wow, this is going to be very interesting," said Scarlet. "Will there be a hostess that will present the food? If so, they should wear their cultural garments."

Here's another idea, they should have their cultural music playing within their booths. There should be small tables with sets of four chairs at each table, if someone would like to sit and eat. Better yet, we could setup one round table that sits eight to a table," said Scarlet.

... Scarlet kept shouted out more ideas

"The hostess should explain the culture and what types of food that is being served, also the meaning of the food that they are serving, why and when they eat their particular dishes."

Scarlet laughs ... "I'm full of ideas today"

Ruby also agreeing with Scarlet's ideas (by shaking her head), "Yea, which sounds like a real good idea Scarlet and very informational," said Ruby.

"You are so right, that's why we called on you ladies" said Natalie, we're looking for good ideas that will wow the crowd and bring them to our side." We want to win that trophy, to go along with the others" as, she pointed to the other five trophies that sat so neatly in its glass case.

"Well, let's hope that they also have ice cream," laughs Ruby "that will sure drive them to your side."

"I'm sure all the restaurants will have ice cream or some sort of cold dessert," said Natalie. "It would be disasters for no one to not, have it … it is the summer!"

"Yea, … Ruby just became a finger waver. But will they have South African or West Indies ice cream," asked Ruby, "They will have to come bigger than that."

"No, I guess your right about that, we'll just have to see what the Chefs are making.

Right now, where are in the beginning stages, but I'll make a note of all of what we're discussing and present all your ideas to the owners," said Natalie.

"Ok, so this is the plan, we know what types of ethnicity groups are coming, we'll present their countries color for the theme along with their country's artifacts, which would go well with the theme. We'll need to type up some numbers, create invoices and get back to you," said Ruby.

"As always thank you," said Natalie "please get back to me right away, so that I can present all of your wonderful, creative ideas to the owners, which in return, they'll have the expense ready for the cook off, well, in enough time to get started."

"Sounds great, I'll have Bridgette get back to you within a week with all the details," said Ruby.
"Wonderful, I'm so excited to be working with you ladies once again" … while getting up from the meeting with the Divas, Natalie said, "Will you ladies be staying for lunch?"

Both mentioning that they had other meetings to attend but would love to take lunch with them.

"Great, it's on the house," said Natalie. "I'll have your favorite waiter come and take your orders. Have a great rest of the day ladies."

"Thanks, Natalie," said Ruby

While waiting for their salads, Scarlet said to Ruby that she was in contact with Bernadette in Paris and that they had setup a video meeting on Wednesday of next week at 8 p.m., for thirty minutes."

"Wow, awesome," said Ruby, "I will sure mention this to Me'chelle, so she can present her very best."

Chapter 15

So Many Designs

Ruby informs Me'chelle that, Scarlet had received a call from Bernadette at La'Fea Agency in Paris, and has taken the liberty, of scheduling a video chat, via Zoom on next Wednesday evening at 8 p.m. "Let me add this, they are excited to see your designs," said Ruby.

Me'chelle sat back in her oversize chair in awe struck, "omg! is this really happening! I am so happy that Aunt Scarlet was able to get through. It's one thing being there in Paris, but receiving a call from Ms. Bernadette about Me, Muah" … Me'chelle points to herself, "how cool is that OMG! I am so excited" yells Me'chelle … her voice was loud and high pitched like a cheerleader.

"Well, alright," said Ruby, "bring that same excitement with you at the meeting. You must bring your best baby!" Ruby looking around Me'chelle's room, and said, "You have so many here, how are you going ever figure out which ones that you'll use?"

"I know which ones I want to present, Mom." And the second time she yells out, "Omg!"

As they were talking Scarlet enters Me'chelle's room.

"Hey, you, Ms. Me'chelle, are you excited or what." It took a while to hear from Paris, but we stayed with it and now you have a video chat, all the way in another country!" says Scarlet.

"OMG! Auntie, yes … thank you so much for coming through with this. I'm so ready for this, well, at least I think I am."

She looks at both Divas and said, "You both live out your dreams every day, now I can live out mine."

Scarlet looking Me'chelle straight in her eyes and speaks.
"Your right little lady," … Scarlet shrugging her shoulders, "do you know what you want to present?

Here's a tip though, when presenting your designs. Show them a fierce attitude, show them that you're confident with your designs, show style and charisma. In this game, you have to set yourself apart from the rest, by being different in style."

Ruby, steps in and said, "But remain yourself."

"Without a doubt," said Scarlet, while popping her head.

Me'chelle felt overwhelmed and felt pressure to present more of her designs... well, the ones she had in mind.

"Well, I do have a lot here, give me a little time and I'll get back to you," said Me'chelle.

All the while Me'chelle, was feeling a little nervous, but also wanted to be alone to breathe a sigh of relief. She wanted to get her designs ready for the show and she knew exactly who to call on when she needed to do something.

"Ha ha ha spoken like a real businesswoman," laughs Scarlet, "I guess you get it from your mamma."

Ruby also laughs and said, "I guess you're right." While popping her shoulders.

As they leave Me'chelle to go over her designs, Me'chelle calls her best friend Greetch.
Greetch and Bubbles met in kindergarten and have been friends ever since. She's able to talk to Greetch about anything and everything.

Greetch picks up the incoming call from Me'chelle, "Hey, L what's up?"

"Are you able to come over, like, right now, you got to help me? I'm going to be presenting some of my designs next Wednesday at 8 p.m. at my house. My Aunt Scarlet was able to get in contact with Paris about my designs. They are looking for me to be fierce, bold, confident and stylish. You know how I get. I just felt this overwhelming nervousness. We need to come up with a plan on how I would present my designs, it's not like they're on fabric, just colored sketch paper. I do have something in mind, but I need your help," said Me'chelle.

"Yea, I hear you L," said Greetch, "but, that's a pretty big move, Paris, fashion and modeling, that's like for grownups. You ready for that, they seem to be busy all the time, stress driven all the time ask Greetch?"

Greetch goes on...

"I ask my dad for a lousy two hundred dollars more to my allowance, you would have thought I was in a math class with all the questions on what I plan on doing with extra money."

"I mean for one they're on business trips, most of the time and leave me with the staff. It's not like the staff is going to give me an allowance. But my dad didn't want to hear it, he wanted a break down on why I needed more money."

"There's always a good reason as to why I need more funds, for entertainment, food, personal hygiene items, must I say more?"

Greetch continues talking. "Movies, pizza parties, skateboarding, games and more games, haircuts, clothing, sneakers, I could use more hats and...."

Me'chelle yells into the phone, which startles Greetch, "GREETCH! Are you there, don't zone out on me now, you're going on and on about you, when I need your help today, I need you to come over RIGHT now!"

"I'm on my way," said Greetch and hangs up the phone.

Chapter 16

Mindy On the Job

Mindy came into the office and was introduced to the small staff, Ruby and Bridgette.

Scarlet shows Mindy around the office, she also shows Mindy the design room, which was well kept by Bridgette.

Each piece, each item was color-coded in its place. The room was a large room with extra lighting and housed four large tables.

She turns to Mindy and said, "A lot happens back here; this is where the magic comes alive. If you can see yourself working here. This is where you will need to get familiar with." Scarlet looks at Mindy for a response… Mindy's eyes filled with excitement.

So, Scarlet asks, "How about it, you're hired if you're still interested in the position?"

"Oh, I'm very much interested, I would love to be a part of the event planning family; I would also like to specialize in creating designs for the events. That's my field of expertise," said Mindy.

Scarlet is very surprised by Mindy's assertiveness, she steps back and looks at Mindy and says, "Already you're looking to move up in positions. I love that drive, it will get you far, keep that drive alive, we are... I mean we will be expanding and that enthusiasm will work in your favor."

"So welcome to Diamonds starring The Dime Divas Scarlet and Ruby Crystal," said Scarlet.

Mindy shakes Scarlet's hands and thanks, Scarlet, for the opportunity.

"Let me reintroduce you as my assistant," said Scarlet.

She brings Mindy back to get acquainted with Ruby and Bridgette and introduces her as her assistant.

After Scarlet introduces Mindy as her assistant, which she plans for Mindy, to start work right away.

Ruby and Bridgette welcome Mindy to the team and wish her much success.

Scarlet had Mindy follow her to the conference room, where they held meetings with new clients.

Scarlet wanted to start right on getting Mindy acquainted with the upcoming events.

She said to Mindy, "You will be a part of a fundraising event that will be held at Vested restaurant on Ninth Ave, in a couple of weeks." She gives her a little history on what the event is for. "A local team will be building … I mean, rehabbing a building for a youth center. We'll fill you in with more details to come. We also have a very big event coming up, as well, "Happy Hollow" is another local restaurant, more of a family restaurant, they have an annual cook off every summer. They bring in the whole nine, bands, a carnival a live act show … awe, a number of food vendors shows up and there's this big cook off."

Mindy taking many notes, which Scarlet was pleased to see, because when she's away, where there is a need, she must take charge and know her part as a team member.

….it was a long two hours, with Mindy filling out so many papers.

Scarlet didn't realize how much she had to go over with Mindy. "This comes like clockwork to me, I'm pretty pooped," said Scarlet. "Let's call it a day and we'll go over more tomorrow, okay," asked Scarlet.

"Sure thing, thank you, I've learned so much so far, what time should I be in tomorrow or more like what are my working hours: ask Mindy.

Scarlet said, "I have to confess, I've been getting up a little late, these past few weeks, not real proud of it but it's the truth. Aww so, I would say about 10 a.m. I mean you're welcome to come in earlier and go over your notes. I can ask Ruby if she doesn't mind letting you sit in the design room and watch them at work. I'm sure, Ruby or Bridgette wouldn't mind, you never know they may put you to work and the hours that we are open is from

7 a.m. to 7 p.m., Monday through Saturday and we do hold special event hours."

"Before leaving out, let me show you where you'll be sitting."

Scarlet takes Mindy to her work area, which was set up in a cubicle fashion. The cubicle was very large. There were boxes on the floor and some loose paper on the desk, but the cubicle and desk still look to be clean.

Mindy looking around.

"Thanks," Mindy said. "This is one of the largest cubicles that I have worked in, I think I will come in early and get more acquitted with the shop and get my desk all set up."

Scarlet shakes her head in agreement and said, "I will have these items removed out of this space before you come in tomorrow."

Scarlet also said, "Let me show you where my office is located."

Mindy stood in the doorway of Scarlet's office, which was not far from her cubicle. She walks into Scarlet's office and stands there admiring all of Scarlet's pictures that hung on her walls. Most of the pictures, were of Scarlet in Paris and one that stood out was of Scarlet in a classroom setting, she was wearing a lab coat.

Mindy asks, "If you don't mind me asking, what were you doing in this picture, wearing a lab coat."

Scarlet mentions she was on vacation and one of her tours was to sign up to make perfumes and lipstick. "I loved the experience, which is why I stuck with it to this day and that was over seven years ago. You're not the only one that asks, everyone that comes into my office and asks about that same picture," laughs Scarlet.

"Wow, I've heard that you travel abroad," said Mindy.

Scarlet said, "You must have heard that from Judy."

"Yeah, but she didn't mention that you were into making perfumes and lipstick," said Mindy.

Scarlet chuckles, "More like, I have a lipstick line called Scarlet Kisses I didn't go with the perfume. Just stuck with the lipstick."

"No way, your Scarlet Kisses. You need to put a face on your brand. I love some of the new shades that have come out this year… it's still a brand-new line, but wow," said Mindy.

"You're correct, I'm still in an early stage of my lipware, it's going on five years now. I'm constantly promoting the lipware and my face can be seen at fashion events, but I like that idea, I'll have to see how I can add it in a commercial. I liked making lipstick so much, that I started to invest in that field two years after I went on that trip, it changed the course of my life as much as the event planning business has, which was passed down from Rose, my mom. You'll meet her sooner or later."

"I have been in Paris for some time now, it's like my second home, getting my lipware on the production line, there are models that wear my line of lipware. I haven't been here in the United States promoting it as hard as I have been across seas, but soon and thanks for the feedback," said Scarlet. Scarlet shrugs her shoulders and lets out a big sigh. "I'm pretty much done for the day." Scarlet looked down at her watch. It's 3 p.m.

"Awesome, well, thanks again for this huge opportunity," said Mindy, while Scarlets shows Mindy out.

"If you don't mind, I would like to say goodnight to Ruby and Bridgette."

"Not at all, be my guest," says Scarlet... Scarlet walks Mindy back to the design room.

Ruby and Bridgette, were both at work, working on the Happy Hollow food ethnicity themes in the design room.

Mindy stood in the doorway and said, "Goodnight, ladies, see you tomorrow morning."

"Good night and congratulations again," said Bridgette.

Ruby smiles at Mindy and waited for Mindy to be out of the event room. She smiled at Scarlet who looked back at Ruby.

Moments later...

Ruby goes to meet Scarlet, in her office, but Scarlet was seeing Mindy out of the building. Ruby stood in Scarlet's office, waiting for her to return.

When Scarlet enters her office, Ruby said, "You seem to be pleased with Mindy. I have not seen you take up so much of your time with anyone, other than your friends, and of course, your glam squad. Something about her, you like."

"Yes, I am happy to have her as my assistance." She walks to her desk and plops herself in her recliner chair, turns on the massager on full blast and closes her eyes, she opens one eye and points as she whispers. "I need just fifteen minutes and you wait; Mindy is special, she has a quality about her, that is going to bring in so much energy into the event center, mark my words." Scarlet takes a deep breath and relaxes her shoulder and lets the massager do its job.

Chapter 17

Video Meeting

It was the day of the meeting, all seem to go smoothly for Me'chelle until she gets home from school and as usual, she heads to her room with a snack in hand, but before getting there she trips over her kickball. "Yup, she's on a kickball team called The Raging Giants." She notices some loose papers under the oversize chair that she always lounges on.

To her surprise, she notices that it was one of her lost designs, that she's been looking for, for about a month. It was not a finished product, but she liked the design. An emerald green, long, flower design skirt with a matching halter top, which connects to the top of the skirt.

So, she retrieves the item, not remembering how it got there, but wanting to present it at the meeting, she had about five hours before the meeting was to begin.

By now Me'chelle was again feeling nervous and not sure on what design to use, after going over the scene with Greetch. The night before, she was feeling hopeful but now doubt was setting in. She was unsure if she could pull this off.

As she walks into the room, Me'chelle appears to be getting more upset, with herself, her desk being a mess with so many designs on it, and not sure which ones she was going to use.

Was Me'chelle having second thoughts?

She became frantic and overwhelmed as she kept looking at her desk and yelling at herself. "You have to clean this mess!" While looking around the room and not knowing what was trash and what to keep (this was Me'chelle second time feeling the pressure of designing) she wanted to be ready and for it to be perfect. Me'chelle and Greetch had gone over her routine more than enough times.

Me'chelle was thinking, *"If Ms. Bernadette does not like my designs. It will be a setback and we must start all over again, finding a designer that will work with my designs."*

Carlotta is the family seamstress, but she's been so busy lately with finishing school and with a laundry list of clients and the growth of her brand Carlotta Designs.

She's done work with me, and we work well together.

Me'chelle says, "I don't know, my G'Ma was right, responsibilities are a pressure cooker."

Me'chelle shakes her head and yells at herself trying to motivate herself. *Stop it, you're too young to be this nervous, think of it as a game, you're challenging your friends to a game of chess... omg! I don't know how to play chess* thought Me'chelle, *ok, ok, ok a kickball game!*

She laughs at herself and got herself together, feeling a sense of confidence, she goes to remove items off her desk so she could finish working on her lost design, which she loved that design and thought it was worth presenting in the video meeting, that evening.

Chapter 18

Me'chelle The Designer

Me'chelle's family, along with Ruby's research team and a handful of Rose's staff, along with Bridgette and Mindy, were set to attend the private fashion show, held on Wednesday evening at 8 p.m.

The setup.

Me'chelle and Greetch, had arranged the room, with strobe lights that lit up the room the kind of strobe lights that flashes and has a misty fog of smoke coming out the lights. Kind of reminds you of a disco 1980's party, with lights flashing and a misty fog filling the room, while everyone dancing, having a good time amongst each other.

Maybe the two (Me'chelle and Greetch), had done some research and found that the setup scheme, would go well with a modeling event.

They had also placed in the room, four brass poles, they had attached a thin wire onto the poles. While the music played, the lights would flash, and the misty fog would fill the room. The wire held Me'chelle designs, and each piece would spin on its axel, as she spoke of the fabrics and her choice of color the design would be made in. She would share about ten items during the private fashion show. She had practiced the stage setting for three days, which they believed and felt confident, that the setup was fantastic and would go as planned.

Promptly at seven-thirty, the doors to the media room open and each guest enters the room to find that there was assigned seating, with name tags on each seat. They seem impressed by the view on their faces... Me'chelle thinking, *I learned from the best.* While they waited for the meeting to begin, they provided their guest, a small portion of refreshments, that consist of cutup hot pockets, fresh fruit cups, and a platter of mixed cookies, they had on ice, mini cans of 7up soda and bottled water.

There was small chatter amongst the guests, each admiring the room and looking at the designs that hung on the brass wire. I'm sure they were thinking about how this twelve-year-old got these designs done.

Seven fifty-five p.m. Me'chelle nervously waves and smiles at her guests.

Suddenly, the lights went dimmed and Greetch lowered the music, I (Me'chelle) counted the moment that the video call was to come in. *I could hear my heartbeat. I turn to look at my best friend, which gave me two thumbs up. I turn back and the video call was in progress.*

Fashion show in progress.

I thank everyone for joining the private fashion show and then Greetch slowly started the wheeled axle. I did not want to appear as being nervous, though I was very nervous. So, started slow and tried to be as graceful and smooth as I could. Greetch would stop the axel in front of the guest on the video call, for each guest to get a perfect view of each design. As I presented each design, I would speak about, how I came up with creating the design and of the color scheme, what type of material the design would be made in. I would save my favorite design for the last show. Greetch was advised to add extra lighting to show off my emerald green skirt and halter top set. The skirt had a beautiful silhouette of a white rose printed on the skirt, which would attach to the halter top. Boy, was I proud of that design? The flower was position over the hip that also look like it could have wrap around towards the back of the skirt and flowed towards the halt top.

Overall, the presentation, I felt like, it went well, and I wanted for my design to appear as if a model was wearing the designs. I was shaking in my boots, but I was proud that I got through my first private fashion show.

The lights came on and Me'chelle walked in front of her guest, not to block Ms. Bernadette's view, viewing from the video call. She had for the first time, introduce her brand, Me'chelle Designs and again, she thanks her guest for coming out to view her summer ware.

Bernadette spoke through the video call, clapping and yelling out "Bravo, Bravo, Bravo Ms. Me'chelle, what a great job" and not only that she applauded, but what seem all of Paris applauding. She thanks her guests, for joining in and shooed them off to speak with us in private. The research team was then dismissed from the private fashion show.

We were going into a private meeting.

"I knew that you would bring your best darling," said Bernadette. "I had invited a few girls and boys, from one of my charities, that I sit on the board of directors on. I invited them to witness a young entrepreneur at work, creating a name for herself. Hoping to motivate them.

That presentation will open doors for others and motivate the younger generation. It's not about sitting around with your hands out but getting your hands dirty and working at your craft.

"I love the pieces darling; you're going to do well, you'll be very busy making wonderful, tasteful clothes for the young generation and in due time I know that you will start to design clothes for young adults and older adults as myself." Bernadette arches an eyebrow and smiled into the camera; I'll look forward to seeing the first design that hit the print.

"If you don't mind me talking a little business with you." Bernadette pauses, to which Me'chelle agrees.

"Thanks, darling, for there's so much more that needs to be done before you can get them on print. You would need to meet designers, someone that you feel comfortable working with, one who can help bring out your designs from a sketch to the fabric. You kind of need the same vision. Do you understand what I'm saying darling?" asked Bernadette.

"I do," said Bubbles.

"Great, I would need to talk more with your mom and go over some business detail later. You have a gift darling, keep designing and thank you for sharing. I know you have it in you to be the next young designer," said Bernadette.

Hand waving in the air. "My time is up, onto the next affair! There is a dinner party in my name." She looks into the video and sees Rose sitting towards the back, to which she yells out, "Is that you Rose, it seems like forever, how are you, my darling?"

"Hello, Ms. Paree," Rose chuckles. "I am well and you? You're looking spectacular in that gown." Rose waves her hand, as to send Bernadette off on her way to her gala. "Go and enjoy your evening. I have a feeling; we'll be seeing you soon."

"You are correct about that Rose, we need to set up a meeting, better yet you all will need to come out to Paris (Bernadette was rushing). They're calling my name darling, I have to go, so long for now," said Bernadette.

Once the call went dead, they turn to Me'chelle and congratulated her on a great presentation.

"We did not expect a show like that little lady, you sure have some creative style," said Scarlet.

"OMG! Yes, that was awesome, I did not expect that either. I just wanted you to come up with her own ideas, having your own style, you had the floor all to yourself to show off your talent and you did just that. I'm very proud of my soon to be thirteen-year-old child," said Ruby, while hugging Bubbles.

Rose mentioned that she also was very proud of her. "Oh, let's not forget Greetch here, her stage manager. A job well done Greetch," said Rose

"That's right Greetch," said Ruby," job well done!"

Chapter 19

For the Youths

Gerald and the team of twelve entrepreneurs were pleased with the invitations that the Divas had to drop off at their office.

The Divas had also suggested, creating billboards and posters to be placed all around the city, listing their website for donations.

Weeks had passed by with the fundraising in place.

They did a good job at soliciting for this project. From what was announced at their final meeting, they had exceeded their goal.

Reese, one of the twelve entrepreneurs stood up and said that he had never worked so hard at gathering funds for a cause so close to his major in college.

"This all being a real up-close learning experience for me, never knowing what to expect. Am I going to make the right call, or when standing in the freezing rain, in front of grocery stores selling the idea, that investing in today's youth is vitally important to their success? There is so little money that one can give but when collecting as a whole, is worthy for the cause."

Well-spoken thought Ruby, while sitting in the final meeting.

Everyone was clapping with joy and asking if they could be a part of other renovation projects in the community.

In the meantime, …

Invitations were mailed to the companies that would be investing in the rehab project. The invitation lists up to four guests from each office, to represent them.

The fundraising dinner

Gerald had requested that each company invited, have their table set up branding their name. There were retail change stores, like Macy's, Old Navy, Michael's, Health Insurance Companies, Fitness Centers, Car Dealership, Banks and Fast-Food restaurants… just to name a few that came out to support the youth project.

The Divas were to place on each table a pamphlet, showing a timeline of the rehab. A little token for the invites to take back to their office and share with their employees.

The dinner was set up in a buffet-style, with selected seafood items, prime rib, pasta, fresh vegetables and an assortment of fresh fruits.

The guests knew the menu selections, for the event, which were listed with the invitations.

Sweet red wine was also served to all that wanted to partake in having a glass.

DJ Spinn or any of his DJs could not make it, due to their conflicting schedules, which caused the Diamond Event Center to hire a band to play soft jazz throughout the dinner. They were to take a short break during the allotted time when Gerald and his team were to present the short video of the rehab.

Once everyone was seated and enjoying their dinner. The Divas were instructed to have the band take a short break.

Gerald, dressed in a black bow tie tuxedo and rocking a fresh cut had approached the podium and spoke into the microphone.

He first introduced himself and his job title. He asks each of his team members to stand while he gave acknowledgments and what their position was within the project.

They were called Twelve, and dressed in their finest and stood tall with pride. They were probably thinking … look your best before getting dirty with the demolition and cleanup process, soon to take place.

He gave a special shout-out to the Divas. Acknowledging their success in setting up the event within a few weeks. Gerald let the Divas know that they did a fantastic job, with all their suggestions. He encourages the guests. "Hire them for events, they are awesome, they see your vision and work off that. Sometimes in little time … thank you ladies you made our jobs that much easier with your help, visualizing the project."

The Divas stood and wave to the crowd and thanked Gerald and his team.

He thanked all that came out to support the project. He also knew there had been silent investors, which he thanked.

He had gone into a small speech about when he was a kid and there were few things to do in his community. But his grandmother had created a group called S.W.G. (Science with Gammy), which was held on Thursdays, like an after-school program. There were crafts and easy science projects conducted within the group.

"It gave us something to do, and we all looked forward to going to her house every Thursday, where she set up her garage with tables and all sort of supplies, that she brought with her own money."

"That's what motivates me to do this type of project, to give back to our youth. When you take away art, you take away a culture. I can't sit still with that."

Gerald thanked his guests.

"We could not do this without your support, my team is truly thankful for your dedication and donations to this project."

He informs the guests, there should be a pamphlet on their table showing a timeline of the rehab, also letting the guests know, they would witness a slideshow that they had put together. "You'll see this slide show, sometime this evening," said Gerald.

"Thank you again for your time, for your support, please enjoy your dinner and thank you once again," he says while walking off from the podium.

The band played soft music again.

While everyone appears to enjoy the friendly atmosphere and the music. Gerald and his team of Twelve had gotten up from their seats to mingle with the guests.

Ruby and Scarlet sat in the back of the restaurant in case anyone needed assistance.

As the host previously mention, the dinner party had watched the same slide show that the Divas had watched a few weeks ago, of the rehab of a dilapidated building.

There seems to have been extra footage added to the slideshow, which showed the footwork of the fundraising in progress, which was a great addition, to the slide show.

Overall, the dinner was a great success, which brought in a great number of funds to help revitalize an old home made to be a youth center.

Chapter 20

Company Meeting

As promised Rose wanted to address the companies becoming one.

This would ease the tension of her staff at Crystal Manor.

Sam, Big Eaze's assistant had sent out an email blocking the time of 3 p.m. on each department's calendar. The meetings were to start weekly to discuss the merge process at the headquarters of Big E's Enterprise.

Sam had gotten the green light to have these meetings in Frank's office.

Frank's office was the larger of the six offices that were housed in a three-story building. He first rented space on the first floor. But the company grew and being that the building was an old building. Frank had struck a deal with the building owner and purchased the top floor, after the purchase of the much-needed space, Big Eaze started renovating the top floor. Frank can be found most of the day, in his office, when not out on business travels.

Rose was the owner of **A Dozen Roses,** and her office was in the building, now called Diamonds. A few years later, while dating Big Eaze and them both, accruing business adventure together. She had eventually gotten an office space on the same floor. Her office was located down the corridor from Frank's office.

Rose, Scarlet and Ruby along with Chef Brew and DJ. Spinn, were scheduled to attend the meetings.

Ruby was overheard discussing the timing of the meeting, they were still in the early stages of creating Happy Hollow event themes for each group scheduled to attend the annual cook-off.

"We need all the time that we can get to finish this project on time," said Ruby. "For one we only have one week to have all the details finished and presented to all six restaurant owners. We must get all the items ordered and tailored, and we need to create the banners. We're waiting on the fabric, so Carlotta can get her part out of the way, before leaving out to God knows where throughout the country."

Carlotta and four of her staff, has been traveling the world. She has signed on to major projects through Rose international connections.

Ruby was a little agitated with the hold upon the items.

Scarlet informed Mindy of the weekly meetings she will be attending before leaving out for Paris and that she (being Mindy) would not have to attend until then.

But believe that their support would be vamped up regarding Happy Hollow décor.

"Great, time to get my feet wet and show my skills," said Mindy.

Attending the first meeting.

Frank, aka Big Eaze looked much like a Big Boss, sat behind his mahogany desk, his chair being tall and stout. He needs it, Big Eaze is a tall and muscular man and he said, "This will not be a weekly meeting, we pretty much handle all business on a day-to-day basis and much of the merge should be handled through our lawyers' signing documents, waiver forms, etc., etc."

Rose spoke up and mentioned, "We would need to have positions listed via a company website or visual work board. I have some staff that may be interested in positions in the enterprise."

"Sure," said Frank now looking at Sam to make a note to add a job listing. "Anything else, while we have everyone here?" asked Big Eaze.

Chef Brew said, "Yeah, I need a bigger kitchen, this business is growing like wildflowers. We are expanding and in need of more space."

"Yeah, that's right, we are to sign off on frozen dinners, by the beginning of the new year, if anyone doesn't know, we are now going to venture into grocery stores which we will be stocking frozen food items made by Chef Brew and his crew. Would you like to share the name Brew?" asked Big Eaze.

Chef Brew chuckles... he hates to be put on the spot.

Well, we came up with **Keep'N it Eazy Meals.**

Big Eaze spun around looking at all attending the meeting ... smiling ear to ear.

"Now that's what I'm talking about," said Big Eaze. "We may need to send over a contractor and see if we have some square footage available via the blueprints, instead of moving everyone out... those are my thoughts on that."

Big Eaze looked over at DJ. Spinn and asks, "How you doing, Spinn, were you able to get in contact with JB in Santa Monica?"

"Naw, I've been in the field. There's no time to make calls," said DJ. Spinn. "Look like I may need to get assistance, you know an office manager."

"I would suggest you hire a temp until you are fully staffed," said Big Eaze. "That way you can scout out more help."

"You know that sounds good," said DJ. Spinn.

"I can give you the number to Judy Wright Temp Agency," said Scarlet.

"Cool," said DJ. Spinn.

"You know this was a really good idea, having this meeting. I think we'll need to schedule monthly meetings going forward, weekly meetings may be too much especially us being out of the office much of the time," said Big Eaze with Sam taking note.

"If no one else has any concerns to address. We can call it a day," said Big Eaze.

Big Eaze was ready to close the meeting, but Rose stops him in his tracks.

"When will the job listing be available," asked Rose. "I would like to let my staff know so they can look out for it."

Sam now speaking "I will need a couple days, maybe a week to gather more data and I'll let everyone know who, what and when in each department if there are any room for advancements."

Big Eaze looks around the room and stops at Rose and says, "Is this okay with you?"

Rose nods in agreement.

Big Eaze goes on to close the meeting and said, "Thank you all for taking this time out from your busy schedule, and have a productive day, week and month."

Rose stayed behind, once everyone was out of Frank's office. She said to Big Eaze, "I want in writing, the merge and what the details are in the merge for Diamonds, who was a branch out of A **Dozen Roses** and now Carlotta Designs. These two entities are not a part of Big E's Enterprises. So, I would need to see the logistics on these two merges before signing off."

Big Eaze wipes his forehead and said, "Thanks for clearing that up. I was gonna say, you have that merge in writing when we sign our marriage certificate."

Rose now shows shade towards Big Eaze and said, "Just get it in writing, lawyer or not, I want it in writing and signed." She leaves his office and walks down the long corridor, where her office was located, and shuts her door.

Rose believes that she's building a dynasty in Diamonds and Carlotta Designs, which **AGM** and Scarlet Kisses, also fall under her reign.

Rose continues in deep thought… *If I'm not for the merge I may need to keep them separate.*

Chapter 21

Burst of Energy

That Mindy is heaven-sent. She is a burst of energy, getting Happy Hollow décor together. She and Bridgette work hand and hand like a mother and daughter duet. Bridgette is the laid-back person and Mindy is the fidgety happy child. They know each other's weaknesses and strengths, it's a great match-up to the event center.

The team had to work over a few weekends to finish last-minute details.

The owners were pleased with what was presented and wrote out checks to cover the expenses for their booths.

Carlotta was on board making the culture attire for each booth. She made simple garments (t-shirts and sun visors).

Carlotta has been busy herself; she's hired two tailors and two seamstresses and looking for a bigger place to work out of. There is a need for privacy and adequate space in the back of the store. All business is conducted in the front, which sometimes causes a messy and crowded workflow.

There were flyers handed out at Happy Hollow restaurant, a month before the cook-off and Natalie had placed a billboard near the restaurant for all to see, it read.

Happy Hollow annual cook-off on June 4th thru June 7th from 12 p.m. to 10 p.m. come out, bring your families, and have fun. The carnival will host live concerts and live act shows and a host of games and most of all food booths.

Everyone in the community seems to love carnivals, it's so crowded in those few days.

Meanwhile...

Bridgette had filled the company van with table settings, artifacts, plastic food containers and plastic utensils and paper-ware. They were scheduled to meet at the parking lot by 8 a.m. to set up each booth. Big E's Enterprise party setup crew were to follow with tables and chairs for the six booths.

They hop in the van like they were going on a road trip and Mindy has the music blasting through the speakers.

Ruby mentioned, "Do we have to have that music turnt up to 100 decibels, it's 7 a.m."

Mindy bopping her head. "We're going to a party, I mean a carnival, where there's sure to be loud music, announcers, the rides and games, just getting you prepared for all of that," said Mindy, while yelling over the music.

Ruby sat back and closed her eyes, while Scarlet sipped on her twenty-four ounce of mojo.

Again, Mindy is a burst of energy. Since joining the team, it's been lively at the event center, with her perky attitude.

Her desk is filled with travel pictures across the globe, she's adventurous for sure.

She had sat with Scarlet and Ruby and discussed having a yoga class at the event center, three days a week. "This will not only benefit us at keeping up with our workouts but also add revenue to the business," said Mindy.

The Divas were so busy throughout events they barely had time to keep up with their daily exercise regimen, so, they gave Mindy the green light to have classes in the back closed-in patio. No more than six girls could fit back there.

Neither Scarlet or Ruby could dedicate three days. But got in a stress reliever workout occasionally.

Bridgette welcomes the change as well and joined in on classes.

When arriving, they found parking and unloaded items.

They met up with Natalie, which she instructed where each booth was set up (one after the other). As suggested, they had one round table with eight chairs to a table in each booth. As they set up the booths, which took no more than fifteen minutes each, they were introduced to the chef, the cashier and the hostess.

Shirts and caps were handed out, pamphlets were shoved into hard plastic stands, a handful given to the hostess, which she would hand one out to every patron dining or taking out.

The artifacts created, were banners of each Ethnicity countries flag to hang over their booth entrance and the food counters.

Throughout the day Scarlet, Ruby and their assistant would visit each booth, to make sure that they had all they needed throughout the day. They were scheduled to stay on sight, close to eight hours a day, for any other assistance that may arise during their scheduled time.

While at the carnival, Scarlet had suggested that they all wear their branded T-shirts, advertising Diamond Event Center.

Me'chelle had designed the shirts a while ago, when creating Rose's wedding gown. It was such a hit, that they tried to remember to wear them at all their events. The t-shirt was designed in the color of sky-blue and the name Diamonds written out to look as if it had burst with diamonds. They all were to wear, white fitted skinny jeans and a pair of comfy white Vans sneakers, that were rocked out in diamonds. They all agreed to make that their signature look while attending events. Scarlet had asked Bubbles to create a signature blazer for formal events. They would need to look professional and by adding the blazer, it would add a professional flair to the jeans and Vans.

The time had arrived when they were set to leave the carnival, which they met up with Natalie again, informing her the time they would arrive each day with more supplies, and to fix anything that needed fixing (banners, tables, chairs). They wanted Natalie to know that they were on standby.

With the four-day event, Diamonds were to receive thirty thousand dollars, more this year because of the six booths they had to maintain on a need-to-need basis, for the four-day event.

While at the Carnival, Diamond Event Center picks up more business during the four-day event. From small birthday parties to group outings, there were dinner parties to look forward to and wedding anniversaries.

There were many requests for their services, due to them walking the carnival grounds, for which they had passed out business cards.

Ruby knew that it would boost sales. Due to Happy Hollow organizing the event.

They knew who would attend the carnival and where they would have their booths set up.

The turnout was huge and Happy Hollow won the grand prize. They had more to offer with the six booths and the food being served.

Natalie was also pleased; she saw long lines at each booth. She took pictures and acted as a journalist by interviewing the patrons as to why they had stopped at their booth of choice.

She received great responses and recorded them.

Natalie had planned on creating a newsletter for each company to see and hope it would be a model going forward in their cities.

Chapter 22

A Visitor

Scarlet and Tide have kept in touch with each other over the past year via Skype, Facetime, whatever one was available. To make time away, more memorable, they both picked out postcards based on what they were feeling or doing at the moment of purchase, most of the postcards were based on two couples at the beach or sitting on a bench in the park or on a pier, even in a coffee house.

They would challenge each other on who would write the most handwritten letters, Scarlet found that to be a challenge, trying to juggle time away from work. It wasn't easy, but she would not let Tide think that she was not trying. They share extended weekends occasionally.

Tide was an old fashion kind of guy, a real gentleman, a lady's man; which Scarlet was impressed with his laidback demeanor. She felt very relaxed with him in her presence.

While Scarlet was driving home, one evening, from a long day of planning events. The moon being so bright it lit up the sky, which made her drive, just that much more enjoyable.

She drove into her condo parking garage, getting into her home, was a struggle due to her picking up some groceries, she would make dinner that night for herself. She was in that kind of mood.

After dinner, she sits on her condo balcony... moonlighting, and checking out the sky full of stars, she drifts off into a deep daydream thinking about the one particular day that she and Tide hung out together, most of the evening was on Crane beach, admiring the sunset and digging their toes into the sand.

Tide hugs Scarlet, letting her know that he had enjoyed her company. That evening, they talk about anything and everything, that came to mind.

Tide mentioned that he was not very interested in high-maintenance women, but Scarlet was the opposite of what he had imagined a high-maintenance woman was.

Scarlet is surprised and says, "Oh, explain yourself, sir."

"What I mean," Tide laughs at Scarlet's response, "is that when you walked into the store, you have to admit, you didn't fit in the scenic view, most women around here, wore swimsuits, sun hats, sandals and carry's big beach bags."

"You came in wearing a taupe color short set and your gold jewelry, just a glow on your skin and your shoes, oh, they were not shoes made for the sand, that's for sure."

"My first thought, you either got a flat tire or maybe you were a film director... may be a celebrity or just going to a dinner party, to one of the restaurants or homes on the strip."

"All I thought was, who is this lady, why is she here, she does not fit into this beach life theme."

Scarlet giggles.

"No, I wasn't going to dinner or had a flat tire or even was a film director." Scarlet was bashfully embarrassed.

"Well, what made you come into my store?" asked Tide.

"Well, for one there weren't many stores on the beachfront that had sold apparel, so you did your thing, holding it down. I'm sure you get a lot of people coming in and out on a daily," said Scarlet.

"Your right, I do, but that day was a very odd day, there were not a lot of people coming in," said Tide.

"Good because I got most of your attention," said Scarlet while smiling at Tide.

"But you didn't buy anything," said Tide.

"I knew we had not picked out any sandals for the wedding and knowing my mom, she would have been at all the stores looking for the perfect pair, she's very picky. I saw your store while driving by, when I was going to the beach homes that she had rented on the beach. From looking from the outside, your store looked very inviting; it had a hometown feel about it. I knew

I would make an appearance, before leaving the island," said Scarlet.

"I'm glad you had. I don't think that we would have met," said Tide hugging Scarlet even tighter.

"Yeah," said Scarlet, not wanting to be the first to mention… *what next.*

Tide politely asks, "Where do we go from here? Now that we got to know more about each other. I know that you also have a brand that takes most of your time and you also co-own an event planning company."

"You guys seem to be so busy, when do you ever get time for yourselves?" asked Tide.

Scarlet was feeling a lot more embarrassed, she didn't know how to answer that question.

"Well, aww, (clearing her throat), I mean, aww … I don't know." Scarlet was trying to laugh it off… "Sorry, I have not thought of that. I have been promoting my brand for so long that I kind of forgot about that area of my life… I'm kind of embarrassed to say that," says Scarlet.

"Don't be embarrassed, it's okay, to be honest… being honest, it helps you to recognize areas in your life that may need some attention," said Tide. (Tide smiles a lot)

Scarlet admires Tide's smile; his teeth were so white and lined perfectly. His smile complemented his cocoa color skin and his sandy brown color hair, which was neatly in dreadlocks. She would stare into his dreaming brown eyes and smile.

Sitting on her deck, looking out towards the moon, drifting out over the ocean. Scarlet, realized that she was sitting there smiling.

She picks up her phone and dials Tide's phone number.

Tide sees that it's Scarlet calling in and answers his phone...

"Well, hello my career-driven, lots of things going on lady, how are you this evening?" asked Tide.

"I'm doing well, I was thinking about you while sitting here on my deck, moonlighting," said Scarlet.

"Were you, you mean you weren't in a meeting or hosting an event." Tide laughs, "You wanna meet on Skype?"

"Sounds good, but I was thinking how about you come up to visit, you haven't been here in months, and I'll be going off to Paris in a couple of weeks, we can catch up on so many things that I've been doing," said Scarlet.

"Thought you would never ask, let me finalize some things here with my assistance and I will call you with my flight and hotel information, sounds good," asked Tide.

"Yeah, that sounds good, I hope I'm not taking you away from anything that may need your attention there in Barbados," asks Scarlet.

"Hey, let me worry about that, I think I deserve a vacation or two," laughs Tide.

"Thanks, Tide, I do miss you and can't wait to see you … have a good evening, I'm on my way to sleep. I have a very big day tomorrow."

"You got it," said Tide.

Scarlet prepares for bed… swaying to the lyrics of Lighting and Thunder sung by Jheno Aiko. She drifts off to sleep, singing… what kind of spell you got me under.

Chapter 23

Lomontes' Blueprint

Big Eaze and his investment team were on the hunt to open more restaurants.

They had picked up so many airline miles in search of a new location. From coast to coast, city to city. It was a long and grueling process, which kept Rose alone most of the time running Big E's Enterprise.

She was not in favor of the traveling process but agreed to stay back and run the company in his absence.

Rose had requested Sam to set up weekly meetings. Rose wanted each department to come up with new ideas for their areas. She wanted all to be on board, from management to employees, all having an opinion.

While in one of their scheduled weekly meetings.

DJ. Spinn had mentioned that he was able to get in contact with JB, which he had indicated that he would be able to come up for a visit, staying about a week.

"Okay," says Rose, "what's the plan for JB, did Frank mention what he wanted him to do?"

"No, that's up to me, but at the moment seeing how he lives in Cali, he's just coming in to learn the process, I'll let him make that decision. His current girlfriend works at Lomontes' restaurant," said DJ. Spinn.

"Well, I'm guessing he wants JB to move here and work under you, he does rap, and I do recall that you were looking for a DJ to interact with the crowd. You guys can have block parties." Rose was interrupted by DJ. Spinn.

"Well, yeah, if he does move up here, down the road, I was thinking about having him teach classes, he's enrolled in a university there in Cali, he's studying music," said DJ. Spinn.

Okay," said Rose, "sounds like we getting the hang of this."

"I want you guys to think of ways of enhancing the brand, there are no bad ideas, look at it as we are starting a conversion," said Rose.

"Chef Brew anything new, you're in the food industry, you should have a long list of ideas." Rose smiles.

"Well, we do so much now," said Chef Brew. "But I have in mind a new dish to add to our ever-growing menu, which would go well for breakfast, lunch as well as dinner. That dish being a shrimp and grits cuisine, I'll add a spicy pork sausage with mixed color bell peppers, adding a dash of fresh parsley. Yeah, I think it'll work. The idea came up from one of the employees when visiting New Orleans, they had a similar dish."

"Oh, so not to completely replicate their dish, you add a little twist to your dish?" asked Rose.

"Exactly," said Chef Brew.

"I like it but I'm looking for a new way of branching out in the food business," said Rose.

"Well, it's a different dish, we don't have anything like that on our menu, we are a fine cuisine catering company and with that dish, we are branching out into different cultures. That's just one way of making that particular dish.

Possibly you and your assist could come up with a new dish a week or month?" asked Rose.

"Possibly," said Chef Brew.

Mitch from Lomonte's restaurant had not joined in the first meeting, conducted by Big Eaze. Due to they were scheduled for restaurant week in St. Monica but, had Skype into the meeting and mention that they were still in the early stages of their opening and working out their prior schedules (Big Eaze had scheduled that restaurant to attend cooking events throughout the valley that year), but wanted Rose to know that down the road they would come up with new ideas. He had touched on soon, having a cooking class. He believes that his Chef might be interested in something in that field. "I've noticed him teaching the younger people in the back end of the restaurant on how he comes up with a specialty dish."

"Wow, now that sounds great and exciting if we don't have a problem here, Chef Brew maybe we can carbon copy that blueprint," said Rose.

Chef Brew agreed, "Yeah, that's pretty smart and innovating, which possibly will bring in more revenue."

"When this class was to start up, please add us to that training," mentioned Rose.

She thanks them all for attending the meeting. "I look forward to your progress in the next meeting."

Sam had taken notes to distribute amongst the departments and for Big Eaze to read in his daily emails.

Again, Rose had not asked for Diamonds to join in the meetings, they were still a separate entity. She had not seen the merge papers yet. So, she was keeping them separate as well as Carlotta Designs.

As she sat back in her chair, giving it a great deal of thought. We *will build a dynasty from Diamond Event center and Carlotta Designs, hopefully in good faith, Scarlet and Ruby would need to merge their companies Scarlet Kisses, **AGM** and the new kid on the block Me'chelle Designs*. "Oh my," Rose was excited. "I need to contact the Divas and Carlotta. I just might be onto something here."

Chapter 24

Sea Bisque

While Big Eaze had been in search of a particular spot to open a new restaurant. He and his team, fly the friendly skies, from coast to coast, city to city. He stays in constant contact with Rose... on a stormy raining day he calls Rose.

Rose was trying to get some much-needed peace and quiet, from a long and busy day of work.

She must admit, running Big E's Enterprise by herself, is no piece of cake. While trying to take a nap she heard her phone ring. She thought about letting it go into voicemail, but she gets up, knowing that it could be very important, she is a partner of an enterprise, head pounding and a little dizzy Rose answers the phone in a whisper. "Hello," says Rose.

"Hey, beautiful, how are you and how have you been doing without me?" asked Big Eaze. "I have some good news to tell you, we finally found a new spot to open up our new restaurant."

There was silence on the other end of the phone.

"Hello, are you, their Rose?" asked Big Eaze.

Big Eaze and his investment team had finally found them a new area to open their chain of restaurants. The new location was to be set up in the lakeside district of Laketown, Connecticut.

The city was thriving with new businesses, and they believe that they would have plenty of diners coming and going all day. They wanted to be finished with the setup by late summer or early fall. The restaurant would nestle in a lakeside community, which the lake had housed, large to small motorboats. The community had a laidback, feel about it.

So, I'm guessing you should know by the description, that they were going to be opening a Seafood restaurant, which overlooks an expansive picturesque lake. They were going for a seaside feel.

"Hey, I want you to name the restaurant it's going to be Seafood Restaurant, you okay with that Rose?" asked Big Eaze.

"I guess so," says Rose. "I hope it's not going to be a fast-food place. Facetime me so I can see what the place looks like. So, that I can come up with an appropriate name for it."

"I'll send over a picture in about an hour, the place is kind of messy at the moment," says Big Eaze.

"Why it's on a lake, I'm sure there are boats out on the lake. Is the place abandoned?" asked Rose.

"Yea and in pretty much in grave condition, it's an old abandon building, it looks like it could have been a workshop, a newspaper workshop" laughs Big Eaze. "The windows are old, there's pale blue-chip paint all around the building."

Big Eaze getting upbeat about the vision of the restaurant.

"I see potential in this building though. I was thinking about raising it above the ground and creating a boardwalk feel. I like the pale blue paint, mix some white and gray paint, add huge white double pane windows. The place will look brand new. But I'll have to admit, it's going to take some time though as I said, there is a lot that needs to be brought up to code in this old building."

"With patience, I know it's going to work out well."

"There's other restaurants in the area, but I don't feel a seaside feel about them," explained Big Eaze.

"Ok, you're trying to sell the idea to me, but I'll wait for the pictures, so I can give it a name," said Rose.

"Yeah, soon… how's everything going at home? You keep the ship in shape?" asked Big Eaze.

"Yes, I am and I'm tired, which I was trying to get a little rest when you called. I need it, it's not easy trying to run an enterprise, everyone calls on you twenty-four hours a day seven days a week. I look forward to any quiet time.

Rose continues, "What seems like an everyday occurrence, I hear all day, did you order this, did you approve that, did my order come, did you sign the contract, did we schedule the venue, on and on and on."

"Yup, that's the life I live, we're creating a legacy for the future," said Big Eaze.

"So, you say," said Rose. "Well, I need this rest right now and my head is pounding ok. I will call you once I see the pictures."

"Alright, love you," said Big Eaze.

"Love you too," said Rose, she hangs up and laid back down closing her eyes, which seem to have been for ten minutes and she hears a chirping sound coming from her phone.

Rose looks at her phone and notices the time, she has been asleep for two hours and missed several texts, calls and video calls.

She sees an attachment and opens it first and sees the building that Big Eaze had described.

"Wow, he wasn't kidding with the look of the building." Rose took a few minutes before calling Big Eaze. The building looks to be about a hundred years old. But it didn't take Rose long to figure out a name. So, she calls Big Eaze, and he answers right away.

"Hey, love, you must have been really tired. I sent the picture thirty minutes after we hung up," mention Big Eaze.

"Yeah, I must have, but I got a name for the building **Sea Bisque.** You should not raise it though. You should complete it as you previously mentioned, painting it pale blue adding, large white double pane windows. I would make sure that the wood throughout the building inside and out looks thick, not that thin wood. The front door should look like a French door but using only one, not double, add a crystal doorknob.

"The building is large enough not to add an addition to it, I think it would take away the old-time feel, I mean you did say that you're looking for a seaside feel. I would also add white frosted cover lanterns for the outside lighting. I'm not sure what it looks like inside so I can't give any advice on it," mention Rose.

"Look at you creating your new seaside place," mention Big Eaze. "You would have to come down for a while and design the inside."

"I don't think it would take long, about a week after getting an interior designer in the area. We'll give them our vision and he or she would create it from that," said Rose.

"Ok, first thing in the morning, I will Facetime you and walk through the building and if you're still interested, remember, you're a partner in this as well, and we need your vision, we'll buy it," said Big Eaze.

"Ok, but how early, I have a 10 a.m. meeting, with the contractors to go over the blueprints for De' Chef place," said Rose.

"Yeah, you can Facetime me if you need me to be a part of the meeting," said Big Eaze.

"Nope, I can handle this, you left me to do this, so I will do it. What, all I'm looking for is extra square footage, which will give

Chef Brew the extra space that he needs. You have the final say," said Rose.

"Well, I would like for you to fly down and get this restaurant up and running, can you do that for me," asked Big Eaze.

Rose does not give him an immediate answer. But went on to say.
"How are we going to handle both of us being away from the enterprise?" asked Rose.

"Sam and I will go into the calendar and see what's ahead," said Big Eaze.

"Well, I have to get back to the office. I'm sure! There are some pressing issues, which need to be addressed. Talk to you tonight," mention Rose.

"Try to have a good day my sweet Rose," said Big Eaze.

Chapter 25

Welcome to The Fold JB

JB had finally taken the extra time away from school and his job. For the next two weeks, he planned on hanging out with DJ. Spinn and when arriving that morning at Big Eaze's studio, the crew immediately was rolling out to a spin competition—hosted by their very own DJ. Spinn.

JB placed his bag in the back of DJ. Spinn's black Chevy Suburban hops in the back with a few of the other DJs that were partaking in the competition, and they rolled out.

Rose had insisted on each of Big E's Enterprise entities to bring in fresh and new ideas, to enhance the brand.

DJ. Spinn was sitting on the idea of hosting a spin competition. He finally took the risk and brought it to the forefront. He believed that he would find his next DJ, to join the fold.

Rose and Big Eaze were for the idea and spotted him the reward money and security detail.

Spinn was responsible for getting the permits for the area he wanted to host the event. He lucked upon an abandoned warehouse, which was listed for sale. However, it took some time, getting the permits signed off.

But after the long process of securing a place to host his event, everything was finally coming into place, and he planned on hosting the first spin competition in the empty parking lot of a warehouse.

The Divas took extra measures and had security line the facility. They brought in food trucks with all sorts of food from De' Chef Place to be sold at the event.

After getting the grounds in tip-top shape for the Spinoff, they lined up ten tables, side by side for the DJs, with 1980's banners of hip-hop graffiti to wrap around each table.

The Divas had come up with a 1980 theme spin-off slash block party and it took little for DJ. Spinn to agree. He welcomes the idea, seeing how Ruby was involved.

The event would be televised, so they were looking for a huge turnout. Big Eaze and his investment team (brothers) had flown in from Connecticut for the event.

Big Eaze was putting the newest restaurant on hold for a few weeks. But before leaving out from Connecticut, they hired several contractors, one being a contractor to gut out the restaurant to add new wood and flooring throughout the building. In addition, they brought in an electrician to rewire the place, which would need to be brought up to restaurant codes designed by the food industry. Rose had requested that when installing windows, that they be floor-to-ceiling double pane windows throughout the building. They had not scheduled an inspection but will do so after returning to the new location. They still had in mind to have their new establishment open by late summer or early fall.

Big Eaze was determined to have most of the grunt work completed or set on a schedule to be completed before Rose was to fly down and complete her portion of the renovation.

He knew they would need to sort out the enterprise monthly calendar before returning to Laketown, Connecticut. Big Eaze was a part of a load of investment deals. From the look of things, there were meetings lined up day to day, week to week, month to month.

Rose was happy to see Big Eaze. They would be putting in place, a third in command while Rose was to go back with Big Eaze to set up **Sea Bisque** Their new seafood restaurant on a picturesque expansive lake.

For some reason, Rose was excited about this project; once again, she had been given full range with no interruptions on designing **Sea Bisque**. She eventually thought it would be best if Big Eaze stayed home while she flies out to Connecticut and start renovating the restaurant, not in its original state or color as she previously had mentioned to Frank. Rose was jotting down ideas wanting to add a touch of elegance off the lake.

Rose had envisioned **Sea Bisque** as an elegant seafood restaurant, the building would be painted black instead of blue. She wanted the inside to be a tannish color with black tables and chair seating. She wanted to also incorporate the same seating outside to match the inside but have umbrellas for privacy and much-needed shade for those sunny days off the lake.

As she searched in designer magazines, she ran upon ground \ lights, which she had also wanted to add recess lighting, throughout the property. She wanted **Sea Bisque** to be a hopping and trendy restaurant for all age groups. Her vision was to portray a warm atmosphere of families having dinners. Corporations coming in for luncheons and dinner parties. She thought it would be great to see first dates coming into wine and dine. Rose was determined to make sure that, their restaurant off the lake, was a beacon of light for boaters and patrons, up in down the lake. Her plans on what she had envisioned for **Sea Bisque**, were all written in her journal of books, which she continues to keep close to her.

The spin-off event was to begin at 2 p.m.

Spinn jumps out of the truck and stands in front of the warehouse, looking at it for a moment.

Ruby walks over to Spinn and said, "I know you're not thinking what I'm thinking."

Spinn turns to face her and says, "So what are you thinking, Ms. Ruby."

"That you should've brought the warehouse and we could've hosted the event inside."

Spinn chuckles and said, "Exactly what I was thinking."

"I was so pumped up from finally finding a huge enough space and signing all those permits. I know it's going to be a huge turnout.

I saw people talking about it on social media. We have ten committed participants to partake in this spin-off."

Spinn looked baffled and mentioned to Ruby, "When it comes to this line of business, we think alike. That should count for something."

Ruby said, "True." And walks off.

The tables had been set up by Big E's Enterprise moving team.

Bridgette and Mindy were fast at work putting the banners on each table. They wanted to be out of the way when the other DJs were to pile in and set up their stations.

Scarlet and Ruby set up the judges' table, which they were asked to be a part of the judging panel.

JB was helping DJ. Spinn set up their team station. Spinn asked JB to handle the huge speakers that also came in with the tables.

JB goes to the truck, where he retrieves the speakers. First, he rips off the bubble wrapping from each subwoofer. Then, one by one, he puts them on a large utility cart, heads to their station and runs back to get another one. He took about thirty minutes to complete all four Bose sub-woofers.

DJ. Spinn was a huge fan of the Bose product and had a lot of their merchandise. His dream, to have a stable place to host his events and purchase items that he does not need to break down and move.

The team worked like clockwork to get things set up and just like that, DJ. Spinn put on some music. He plays Da Baby, Rockstar. I guess he was feeling like a rockstar after having that special moment with Ruby.

The food trucks were arriving. They pick their spot, and the smell of cooked food was heating up an appetite.

Ruby noticed cars being park in the designated parking area and people getting out with equipment. She informed DJ. Spinn that she believes competitors were coming to sign in.

There also was a process to be admitted to the competition. There would only be ten competitors.

Ruby greeted each competitor and directed them to DJ. Spinn to sign in. After their admission, they were ready to set up their tables.

Each competitor was given a number to wear around their forearm.
The time was getting close to 2 p.m., and no one seemed to be making their way into the event, but the show must go on as planned.

Each competitor was to start exactly the time given to them.

.... 2 p.m.

The first DJ started on time and the judges sat in their seats, ready to judge each DJ.

About 2:15, more cars filled the designated parking area, with security directing the traffic. Some people stop to get food and beverages before joining the competition.

The first DJ was just about to close when he mixed some electro and bass music. He had the small crowd yelling with excitement.

As time went on, more people were filling in. We were now on the third DJ.

By the fifth DJ, we hit the capacity level. Spinn was informed that security had to turn people away.

By the sixth DJ, the crowds were dancing, some in groups that gather, attempting line dancing.

It was getting hot, with lighting and the equipment's, generating heat and the crowd being so large.

Bridgette and Mindy had turned on tall fans, which were placed all about the empty lot. The fans gave off such a wonderful mist of cool air.

Things were finally whining down, now on the last DJ, numeral Uno number 10, who seemed to bring it much harder than the rest. He brought more to the game, with him rapping, which got the crowd pump. He was mixing the latest and the past music, like Biggie smalls and much of Tupac music.

DJ. Spinn barked out inspirations throughout the event, which made the crowd go so hard on all the DJs, making it that much more difficult to judge each DJ.

But in the end, we all chose the tenth DJ.

DJ. Spinn announces his name to the waiting crowd. "I like to present the winner of the first, but not the last of these competitions, a newcomer to the city. From the valley of Saint Monica, let me introduce you to my man JB."

He received a trophy, which he pounds towards his chest like... Yea, I'm the champ! He also was awarded a thousand dollars.

See JB got in on the competition due to the tenth DJ never showing up and DJ. Spinn also wanted to see what he had, and boy did he bring the noise.

Big Eaze said, "I told you, I got an ear for that type of stuff." He did get the credit for JB coming to visit.

They party for another hour or two with the crowd and JB and the other DJs mixing the music.

The event was over at 8 p.m., and surprisingly, each person helped clean up the lot and security stayed until the last person got in their cars and left the area.

Before leaving the lot.

DJ. Spinn and Ruby stood in the same spot they stood when first arriving. DJ. Spinn turns to Ruby and said, "I'm glad I stepped out and took this risk. This was an awesome event and you know what, I'm feeling good, so I'm buying the building." He went on to mention the distance of where the warehouse was located. "It's not too far out, a couple of miles from the city. We can get people out to a party and, while not in use, rent the space."

"Or spaces, all depending on how you have the space set up," mentioned, Ruby.

"Yeah, true dat. What you think about that," (in his Native New York accent voice), asked DJ. Spinn.

"I think it's awesome and a very good investment move," said Ruby. "I'll get the papers ready for you to sign first thing in the morning."

"Wait, what, you own the building?" asked Spinn.

"Yup," said Ruby while walking to her car. She opens the door and gets in.

DJ. Spinn follows, shaking his head in disbelief. He leans in towards Ruby's car window to ask her, "Can I at least buy you a drink? It's still early." DJ. Spinn points at his watch.

Ruby mentioned, "There's no room for business and pleasure in my book, so I'll decline... well, at least until you buy the building."

DJ. Spinn was ok with that because for the first time, Ruby smiled at him and he felt it was genuine, which he took as they were finally moving in the direction, he had so patiently been waiting for... a real date.

DJ. Spinn mentioned, "I'll see you about 10 a.m., where should I meet you at... Ms. Mogul investor?"

"My office at **AGM** is located on," and she recites the address to DJ. Spinn.

"See you then," said Ruby.

Chapter 26

Hey: don't forget about me

With everyone doing their own thing, Me'chelle felt as if her dreams of becoming a designer were being put on hold or, what it seems to Me'chelle, being pushed back to the wayside. But she refuses to be ignored.

She sits at her design table and designs more each day, but not having heard from Paris or her Aunt Scarlet, on what's next, Me'chelle was becoming concerned.

She continues to stuff more of her creative designs in her notebook of designs. She keeps up with designing sweaters, pants and more skirts and lots and lots of dresses, long and short, some come in printed designs and others are made in vibrant colors of spring and warm colors of the fall. She thought to create a winter line. She's added fur, too much of her winter wear.

One of Me'chelle Designs, models in a skinny fitting to the knee skirt, a (pencil skirt), is seen, wearing a turtle mock neck sweater, all being in white. A winter white, as most would say. The drawing shows the model posing with one leg out in front of the other, in a fierce stance, rocking a mid-level winter white pea coat, which came with a fur collar—the model swings over her shoulder a cheetah-printed diamond incrusted purse with matching knee-high boots.

Being at such a young age, she is very serious about her designs and very much interested in getting them on fabric. She continues to want to see her design labeled as Scarlet Kisses.

She hasn't mentioned that yet, but soon she will be heard.

While the family was having their usual Sunday dinner at her G'Ma's house, Me'chelle felt this was the perfect time to speak out.

As she prepares to speak, she clears her throat. "Excuse me." While pointing at herself she says, "Yea me, tada Me'chelle, did you forget about me, the youngest in the family, the inspiring designer."

Everyone stops talking and turns and looks in her direction.

"Hi," said Me'chelle smiling, while all eyes seemed to peer down at her.

"I just want your direct attention and this being the perfect setting, dinner." Me'chelle still smiling.

"It's been a while, well, feels like months has gone by, that muah (points at herself) had a fashion show and Paris was in attendance of that show ... that counts for something, being in the fashion world, wouldn't you say that to be true, Aunty?" asked Me'chelle.

Scarlet started to agree, but Me'chelle continued.

"Let me see if I can get this right," said Me'chelle.

"G'Ma owning Carlotta's Design, spearheaded a **Dozen Roses** now called Diamond Event Center and partner of Big E's Enterprises."

"Mom owns **AGM** and a laundry list of properties as well, her name is attached, to a host of patents." Everyone looks at Ruby. "And co-owns Diamond Event Center."

"Aunt Scarlet owns Scarlet Kisses and fly's out of the country what seems like every three months, promoting Scarlet Kisses and she also co-owns Diamond Event Center."

"Big Eaze, aka Frank, owns Big E's Enterprises."

"Soooo." And Me'chelle twirls her head looking at this picture. "Where do I fit in? I've been waiting to take off in my career. Yeah, I'm young, but I have a talent I believe most of you agreed was worthy of investing in."

"I feel as if I'm not being taken seriously. But I am so very serious about this." Me'chelle's palms hit the table.

Me'chelle spoke as if she was conducting a business meeting.

"I'm not saying that you have truly forgotten about me, but I am saying that I haven't seen any movement towards my way."Me'chelle, now having their undivided attention, even the staff stop to listen to her speak. *"Wow,"* Me'chelle thinks. *"This feels great, everyone is paying attention to me speak about what my interest are, this feels powerful."*

Ruby spoke first and mentioned, "I don't believe we forgot about you sweetie, we've been so busy."

Me'chelle cuts in and said, "Don't I know… like busy with your own careers."

Scarlet steps in and said, "Bubbles…" (Me'chelle's eyes said it all, like to say, *really)*

"Sorry, but you will always be Bubbles to me, but I respect that you want to be called Me'chelle, so again, please accept my apologies."

"Yeah, I want to be taken seriously," said Me'chelle and she pulls out her book of designs (so many of her designs were in that book) and places it on the dining room table, for all to see what she's been up to.

Rose picks up the book first. She opens the book and you guessed it. She saw the lady in winter white…

OMG! thought Rose, *this is gorgeous, a night out on the town lady, very classy, a real fashionista lady, much a Boss lady in the Fashion world and she is fierce.* "I want this!" yells Rose.

Rose continues to look through the book while they all were trying to peek.

Ruby assures Me'chelle what she means. "We, have not forgotten about your dreams of becoming the next top young designer."

"Yes, sweetie," said Scarlet. "In this field, it takes time and when the time presents itself, then you move in like a lioness and take it by force. Remember what Bernadette had mentioned, that we would need to find a designer that works well with young designers that would help bring out your designs."

"What would they need to bring out, I'm designing them and I think they are right for the world. I need a team that will work with me, creating them in real life," said Me'chelle.

Again, everyone stood still and was puzzled, like is this correct, is she twelve years old or thirty years old? Was she speaking as a young entrepreneur would speak to a crowd of onlookers? They were truly surprised, and their faces said it all.

"I have an antidote for that," Rose blurted out, now everyone was looking in her direction.

"My granddaughter is correct. I sit as CEO under several entities, and with that, I would like to have a meeting to come together and go over some ideas that have been burning in my head while managing Big E's Enterprises in his absence.

"If we are in favor of a meeting," said Rose. Rose looks in the direction of Scarlet and Ruby. She spoke to them directly. "Scarlet, Ruby and you to Ms. Me'chelle and I will also reach out to Carlotta. Let's meet and brainstorm, perhaps sooner than later. I still have to fly out to Connecticut to help design the interior and the exterior of **Sea Bisque**."

Big Eaze looking at Rose in a bewildered state of mind… like, what are you talking about.

More like what am I up to, thought Rose was looking back at Big Eaze all while smiling within.

You can see the suspicion in Ruby's eyes, and she said, "Ok."

She, too, was ready to spearhead her daughter's dream of becoming a designer, taking the steps in helping Me'chelle take her sketches off the paper and add them onto fabric. But Ruby was also being a little skeptical. She doesn't want Me'chelle to get wrapped up in designing and she hadn't finished school.

"I'm also interested to know what you have in mind," said Scarlet.

Rose now sits back and thinks, "*Now is where we **Build a Dynasty.***" Bobbing her head and smiling in agreement with herself.

Me'chelle, viewing the faces of the powerful career-driven family members around the dining room table, was pleased that her voice, her concerns, were finally being heard. Me'chelle was thrilled that she spoke out, *like Aunty said, take it by force* and smiles within herself.

Chapter 27

All Business

Rose got in contact with Carlotta, who has been working out of the country for some time now. She had agreed to Facetime into the meeting and Scarlet, who had flown out to New York City on a business connection.

Mindy, Scarlet's assistant, had lots of connections in the Big Apple. She convinces Scarlet to take a leap of faith. They have both been in the city, close to two weeks now.

Scarlet wanted to test the market in promoting her lipware in the United States and thought what better place than New York City to see how the market would welcome her.

Ruby and Bridgette, as always holding down the fort, but the yoga center is limited to one class a week due to Mindy being offsite.
Me'chelle has been hanging around the event center, helping in Scarlet and Mindy's absence.

Rose does not want to meet at her office but meets at Diamond Event Center.

Rose and Evelyn arrived with dinner for the small group, consisting of a honey glaze baked Salmon, a fresh spinach salad and white wine and water for Bubbles.

Evelyn sets the table while they all gather, ready to meet. One by one, Facetime rings in and Scarlet and Carlotta are connected into the meeting.

Carlotta was in a large room, which showed a wall of color and printed fabric. She greets everyone.

"Hey, Carlotta, how you've been?" asked Rose.

"Absolutely great. Things are moving along well. I'm looking to be back in the states soon, we are in the finalizing stage with the wedding party and once that's completed and the wedding has taken place, we will be back home." Carlotta emphasizes the word *home*.

"Awesome," said Rose. "Please be safe in your travels back to the states."

"Scarlet and Mindy, what's the 411, on the lipware progress, you making any noise, attracting any buyers, lining up commercial airtime?" asked Rose.

"I'm... not sure if that's a joke or not, Mom, but aww, we're, we're being seen. It is kind of moving slower than I anticipated, but we're being seen, and we have some meetings scheduled in the next two days, which I will be demonstrating my product... thanks for asking," said Scarlet.

"Oh, you're welcome. In due season, you will reap a harvest in America. So, hold on and be patient with the market. Hope to see you two soon as well," said Rose.

"Hey, the girls are missing the yoga session, Mindy. They've mentioned that once a week is not enough," say's Ruby.

Mindy giggles.

"I gave the girls a DVD to go over and ask them to be faithful to our class and that I will be back soon. So, I'm hoping that they would honor that agreement," said Mindy.

"Of course, they will. They love your energy. They are waiting on your return," said Bridgette.

"Thanks, Bridgette," said Mindy.

"You're welcome," says Bridgette.

Bridgette and Mindy are truly a heaven-sent pair, to the event center. They work so well together. It's like a burst of sunshine, filling the office with energy. Each day, there's something new to be heard or do. It's a group effort, it's electrifying, which keeps it fun and interesting.

"Well, I don't want to keep anyone much longer. So, let me start with this opening. We are not under the umbrella of Big E's Enterprises, and when I say we, I'm talking about Diamond's Event Center and your businesses as well, Carlotta's Designs and Me'chelle and her designs as she had previously mentioned the name of her company would be **Me'chelle Designs**. I believe I want to keep it that way... well, at least, at this moment. So, we're not in competition, let me get that straight and we still work closely together."

They continue to set up banquet halls, and we have a full range of DJs. This will continue as we do not have a contract set in stone, so, they may not always be available, and we will continue to use their catering staff. This comes with a fee. You can't run a business for free.

Rose cuts to the chase.

"What I see here, around this table... a group of strong women. Now what I am about to say, I don't want it to sound like I'm saying, 'me myself and I,' created this, but you have to admit, that it all branches out from a Dozen Roses."

Diamonds, flourishing in their own rights, under the Divas.

"Carlotta Designs was not created by me but given a huge opportunity to bellow out."

"For the newest person to come into play, is Me'chelle. She started, hiding her talent. She saw her G'Ma, in distress, trying to find the perfect wedding gown."

"She took the leap of faith, over tea and cookies and presented a sketch she had created. She shared the gown she had sketched out for me."

"With that beautiful gown, I hired her to create the entire wedding apparel. I didn't have her make Frank's clothes, but you follow where I'm going with this. She did such a phenomenal job.

She stayed focused, kept me up to date on what was completed. She continues to love what she does and wants her career to start."

"With all of that, I've said, pointing out our talents and our passion for succeeding in our field of interest. I believe she has a real chance of doing the same."

"Ruby, you're an investor, so invest in her start-up, and Scarlet, you've mentioned before, well, I thought I heard you mention you wanted a label. So, Tada, there it is Scarlet Kisses with kissy red lips, labeling Me'chelle's Designs."

"It all boils down to this. I would like for all of us to join forces and create a brand. Creating a safety net of strong women, ready to tackle the world of opposition."

Rose pauses for a moment and then continues.

"I'd like to open the meeting for discussion with any ideas and possibly get some feedback from you. For example, do you see us building a brand or seeing it as far-fetched to become a unified group of strong women building a brand? I'll leave the floor open for discussion," say's Rose.

Ruby chimed in first and mentioned, "I think this is a great idea, but my only opposition towards this is that Me'chelle is still in school. I don't want her to get so wrapped up in demands and deadlines and photo shoots. I'm afraid that she may fall behind in her schooling. But, for God's sake, she hasn't turned thirteen yet. If we can take this slow, then I don't see why she can't spring out in this field."

"I've mentioned that she needs to see what goes on in the background of the fashion world and has the offer to let her shadow with the glam squad this summer in London as well as in Paris," said Scarlet.

"I'm for the unit coming together under one umbrella, I believe, we all have something to bring to this demanding world, which I am truly thankful for the opportunity given to me," said Carlotta. "I love working with you, Rose and the Divas and you to lil chicka."

"So... Ruby and Scarlet, not taking away, from what you two had previously mention regarding Me'chelle. Are you willing to join forces under one umbrella," asked Rose.

"Sorry, yes I am," said Ruby. "I kind of got off base for a moment."

"Likewise," said Scarlet.

"Great, I'm in favor of coming up with a plan of action towards Me'chelle and her schooling. We do not permit slackers in that area. We need to come together as a family unit and discuss unique ways of getting around this matter.

"Back to the umbrella, we would need to come up with a name for the brand. We don't have to come up with a name today, but please keep that in mind, toss out a name from time to time. We still have to make sure to trademark the name," said Rose.

Rose looks around the table and taking notes and said, "Well, this was a very productive short meeting and I thank you all for wanting to hear me out and wanting to come together and create a brand."

"For you three out of towners, please be safe in your travels and shock the world with your love of what you believe in."

"If all are in agreement, this meeting is adjourned," said Rose.

"We're good," said Scarlet.

Carlotta, in a heavy Spanish accent, said, "Gracias"

"Ok, see you all soon then," said Rose.

Scarlet and her Facetime went out.

Chapter 28

Working out the details

Weeks had gone by, and no one could come up with a name for the unifying group of ladies.

While Scarlet was out having lunch with Rose, she threw out a name, hoping that Rose would catch the wave. She says, "How about Rock Solid, for a name." While she looks at Rose for a response.

"Well, we'll need to run it past the team, but it sounds promising," said Rose.

"Yeah, defining Rock Solid would be that we are making an impact on society, with our values, our strengths, our integrity to build character," says Scarlet.

"Wow, now that you put it that way, it makes it sound, that much better," says Rose.

"How about **"Women That Builds,"** we can build on Values, Strengths, Integrity while building character," says Rose.

"Yeah, and it doesn't have to end there. It can go on and on and on, **building**, would be the keyword," says Scarlet.

"Yes, I think we found our name, but I must present it to the others and then fill out the forms for a trademark … I am excited. I love the name," said Rose. "Thanks."

"Oh, yeah," says Scarlet and smiles in agreement.

Rose calls for a meeting with Scarlet, Ruby, Me'chelle, Carlotta would Facetime in the meeting. She would introduce to the group their new group name, hoping they would all be on the same page.

So, she thought to have the name written out, Rose believing that if she showed it as a marketing tool, it wouldn't be so hard to reach an agreement.

She did not want to involve Sam and take her from her duties at Big E's Enterprises. So, she gets Evelyn involved, her assistance.

To create the Women's message, What Evelyn was given was not on a normal sheet of paper. The paper given appeared to be thicker than a normal 8/10 standard white sheet of paper, it was a formal paper that came in the color of beige, and it was lined in gold. The topic read:

Women that Build

Builds in Harmony
Builds on Love
Builds on Strength
Builds on Happiness
Builds on Integrity
Builds with Honesty
Builds with Character
Builds strong Families

Women that Build, Build together!

Rose held up the sheet of paper showing the message before passing it around. She wanted first to see if all agreed with the name. So, she said, how about Women that Build and waits to see a response.

All agreed, which Rose was excited that they came back fast with their responses. She said that Scarlet came up with the topic regarding building on statuses. She then passes around the formal message.

Rose looks at Bubbles and says to her that she was the youngest of the group and may not truly understand the concept of the group but will down the road.

Bubbles mentioned, "I get it. I understand the message."

"Awesome, you are ahead of your time, little lady," said Rose.

"I will petition for a trademark, and we'll work out the other details later, possibly have office space available for this group. We may be looking to have more come on board and participate in events that we'll have down the road," said Rose.

"One event we may want to have, would be a women convention, where we hear from women of other cultures on what their day is like from a day-to-day basis. How could we come together and build a community of strong women, helping with different projects in their community. Whether it be in painting, gardening, or speaking engagements, there could be older women who need help. We would not know it if we were not in their community. We can even have several leaders in their community that they would go to for assistance."

"I think you ladies had a fundraiser a few months ago, where a group of people renovated a building now geared for kids. We could have that in each community. Hopefully, there would be a place that we could work out of. If not, I'm sure we could rent a space. These things, I'm just suggesting. We want to be more hands-on with this group."

All sat quietly, taking it all in and Bubbles mentioned, "Should we have chapters and if so, we would be the first chapter, this way, it would help identify each district.

"Ok," says Rose. "You're not only a designer, but I see that you're in Public Relations as well. Is this something that you're taking up in school?" asked Rose.

"Nope," said Bubbles.

"Ok," repeated Rose looking at her granddaughter.

Ruby just smiled while Scarlet looked at Bubbles like, what does she know about districting.

After Rose closed out the meeting, they all got up from their seat and went on their way.

Later in the weeks to come, several events have called for the Womens' group to be put on a temporary hold, but they were able to get the name trademark

"Women that Build, Build with Character"

Chapter 29

Summing it all up

From Ruby being CEO of **AGM** and investing in properties throughout the city, while Scarlet Pooh comes back in town, from her exhausting lifestyle of promoting Scarlet Kisses also shows concern as to why her soon-to-be thirteen-year-old niece calls her while in Paris on a daily.

.... Breakfast

While discussing business, both Divas meet up at one of their favorite restaurants to dine out on some awesome, delicious, lip-smacking hotcakes.

... Get to it

Ruby starts the wheel in motion to get Scarlet to move faster at getting her assistance. "Like asap!" mentioned Ruby.

...Demand

Ruby knows that Diamonds are in high demand. Therefore, they are requested weekly to host an event.

.... Interview

Right away, Scarlet knows who to call on when she needs some help in picking out the right people. She calls her high school counselor, turned entrepreneur, Judy Wright, and just like that, Judy gets on it, like lightning in the sky. Scarlet has a list of interviewing points that she's retrieved off the Google website.

.... By design

We got a fashionista in the family, Ms. Me'chelle ... aka Bubbles. She sketches just about every day, and she's loving it and wants to label her designs Scarlet Kisses.

.... Run

They all went running to see what Bubbles had sketched. Bubbles wants her designs off sketch paper and on real fabric, on an actual model, to their amazement. Scarlet with connections into the fashion world, makes a call to Paris,

.... Who

The Monarchs are home. There's a chill in the air from their extensive travels aboard, which catches Rose off guard. After loading their relics into their chariot, they're whisked away to their humble abode. With a snap of a finger, they have arrived at their expansive estate.

.... Dinner

They prepare a feast for hungry souls waiting on their return. They gather in their home to eat and be merry. Of course, the guests want to know all about their travels aboard.

.... Rumors

There's a meeting in the lady's room, and the schedule coming out real soon.

Rose's ears are itching. She finds that little mice are running around, creating rumors amongst the staff. So, she doused the fire with bribery... you guessed it, no more rumors!

... Silent investor

For the youths, Ruby quietly sits back in her chair, knowing that she's a part of this awarding winning revitalization.

.... You're hired

Scarlet stands waiting at the door with so much excitement. She wants to introduce Mindy as her assistance to the party of two, that is fast at work.

.... Prior engagements

"You must meet on Monday at 2 p.m." As Bridgette barks off orders, "And I'll take notes like a boss," laughs Ruby. "What's that a fashion show? Oh, I'm with that, food involved, ok count me in."

.... Paris

"Yes, darling, you must say, the whole family is gifted. You and your Glams are missed here in Paris. That it's much quieter since you've been gone," laughs Bernadette.

.... A showdown

Cook-off, Carnivals, food authenticity, should I say more? "Yes, bring on more business!" Both Divas laughing.

... Fierce, Bravery and Confidence

"Show up and show out," says Me'chelle to her best friend Greetch.

.... On the Job

"Oh, you're the name behind the product," yells Mindy as she continues to view the pictures of lab coats and goggles, which adorn the walls in her boss's office.

.... Video

Me'chelle, a kickball gymnast, kicks her ball and finds her lost design, which she wants to present at her video meeting at 8 p.m. tonight. Bravo, Bravo, all of Paris cheers!

.... "The Twelve"

"Restore, Rebuild, revitalize a community by giving back to the future of our youths," said Gerald and the crowd roars with excitement.

"Yeah" yelled Ruby ... knowing she was one of many silent investors on this fulfilling city-wide project.

.... Address the issue

"I like to see that on legal paper and put it on a visional board, so all can see what we're up to," mentioned Rose.

.... Who left the bag out?

"Mindy ran around *and got us all up, trying to match her everyday energy. That girl must take a chill pill*," thought Ruby.

.... Far away

Scarlet sits on her balcony and drifts off, far, far away. Finally, she finds herself with an overwhelming Tide of emotions and calls out.

.... A sitting Queen

Rose demands more of her workers, who seem to be in a state of relaxation, in Big Eaze's absence. Finally, rose yelled out, "Work, work, work, don't you bring me, no more bad news!"

.... What's on the menu

A fine seafood cuisine served by a picturesque lake while boaters were sailing up and down the massive lake.

.... #1 Rapper

He gets to work and wins the three-foot Spin table trophy ... don't forget the loot. Welcome to stardom JB!

.... Hey!

"I will not be dismissed. I will not be ignored, I will not be looked over, I will be heard, I will be recognized, my voice will stir a generation," says the little of the bunch.

.... And the business is

Join forces, join in unity and say no to the nay sayers and they all chanted... ladies first, ladies first!

Scarlet looks down at her mom, stretched out on her lounge chair and shakes her, yelling, "Mom, Mom." Rose awakes and sits up, now looking around and asked Scarlet, "Wow, was I sleeping?"
"And snoring and you also talk in your sleep," laughs Scarlet.

Rose wipes her face and mumbles, "Now that was a dream," she gets up off her lounge chair while singing ... "Ladies first, ladies first!"

Meanwhile, a world of events has come up for the Crystal family.

Chapter 30

Off to Paris

What a sad moment thought Bubbles (she was going away for the summer; she would leave her friends behind for what may be an extended summer) …. Ruby and Me'chelle, were packing their luggage, soon to be heading out to the airport.

Paris called Ruby on business, which was an eye-opening moment for her. She would be interviewed for a chairman seat, under a list of investors, that she has been reaching out to. The Elite, as they are called, travels the country, seeking potential clients, investing in their dreams.

This group of investors comes just under a group of forty. The group comprises of women and men in all age groups and different ethnic backgrounds.

They are called The Elite Investment Group for a good reason. They have invested millions within the group. They are invited to speak all over the country and have kept a close eye on the **AGM** portfolio.

Ruby is excited about this opportunity and looks forward to meeting the group.

For the youngest of the family, Me'chelle, a blessed young lady with loads of talent, has accepted the call, of a demanding, high-energy career, in fashion designing.

Ruby had closed her home and will be ready to sign Me'chelle up in cyber school, if necessary.

Scarlet also, packing for her travels back to Paris, her and her Glam squad were to attend a huge fashion show in London and thought it be best that Ruby and Bubbles also attend the event. So, *I'll get VIP passes for them*, thought Scarlet.

... Rose influence

Scarlet and Ruby took the advice of Rose to back Me'chelle in her fashion design.

AGM invested in the startup label of Scarlet Kisses • 🖊 designer, Me'chelle Crystal.

This would be a big move for them. Starting a label takes time, patience and networking, with the right people.

Ruby's research team, were to stay back in the city, continuing the everyday scanning the globe for potential clients. Instead, Ruby is setting in motion an office manager to help with everyday business.

... Diamond Event Center

Bridgette was now the Lead Event Coordinator and Mindy was her assistant.

They were now in charge of the events in place for the next eight months. They were to schedule weekly video meetings with Scarlet and Ruby.

Carlotta had finally arrived back in the state (well, for a little while), she had also offered her assistance, Carlotta mentioning, "If there's a need, why did I even say that? There's always a need in the event business."

Rose overseeing the event center, from Big E's Enterprise, had planned on hiring a team to help with the events and thought it was fit to hire four employees.

Scarlet gives Rose the name of Judy Wright's temp agency for potential employees and hands over her interview questionnaires. She said, "You may want to use this list of questions."

"Thanks," said Rose. After viewing Diamond's eight-month calendar, Rose plans on calling Judy's temp agency right away.

As she viewed the list of interviewing questionnaires, Rose asked Bridgette and Mindy to sit in through the interviewing process scheduled after hearing from Judy Wright Temp Agency.

... the time is near

As Scarlet, Ruby and Me'chelle, get ready to leave for Paris, Me'chelle asks her G'Ma, "Will you not be coming with us to Paris? I need my #2 girl with me, cheering me on."

Rose sits with Bubbles to assure her that they (meaning her and Big Eaze) will not be too far behind them. "Don't you worry, we'll be there soon, sweetie. In your mom and auntie's absence, I need to hire some people to help out at the event center."

Me'chelle seems ok with her G'Ma's answer. So, she gives her G'Ma a big hug and tells her she will miss her and already cannot wait to see her.

Rose gently cups Me'chelle face and lets her know that she will miss her as well, and lands a kiss on her forehead.

Rose walks into the living space, where Scarlet and Ruby were waiting on their Shuttle, to the airport. Rose looks at them and mentions that she will miss them, "Take care of my lil love bug." While hugging Me'chelle.

While they continue to wait for Big E's Enterprise shuttle, Rose is concerned about how Ruby would be getting around Paris while she conducts her business, so she asks, "Ruby … how will you be getting around Paris while Scarlet is at work and Bubbles in school?"

"Taxi," laughs Ruby. "I do know that the Elite team will have transportation for me for my first day of meeting them. After that, I am not sure, but I'll figure it out, don't you worry."

"What is this," interrupts Scarlet. "Are you getting separation anxieties or something?"

"Just a concerned parent," laughed Rose.

Evelyn comes into the living space to let them know that their ride has just arrived.

Rose looked at their luggage and asked, "Where's all your luggage."

Ruby mentioned that they just had one luggage apiece and, if they needed anything else, that they would purchase all they needed in Paris.

They all hugged Rose and Big Eaze and shuffled their selves to the shuttle. The attendant took what was given to him and loaded their luggage, while Scarlet, Ruby and Bubbles got into the shuttle and said their goodbyes while the shuttle door closed.

Rose became very emotional. You can see that her eyes were filled with tears while waving goodbye. Then, she watched the shuttle leave Crystal Manor, turn onto the street, and was out of sight.

Evelyn was seen with tears in her eyes while they all walked into the home and sat in silence.

After an hour had passed, Evelyn asked Rose, "What did she have in mind for dinner?"

With so much sadness in her voice, Rose said, "Awe, I guess my usual, a blackened sea bass salad."

"Would this be the same for Frank?" asked Evelyn.

"I would say so." Rose still in a somber mood but wanted to know where Frank had disappeared to. He was out of site after the girls had left out.

Rose went in search of Frank and found him in his home office, with his phone in hand and his laptop open.

He turns to look at Rose, who was standing in his home office doorway and said, "I'm searching for a building, we need to buy a building in Paris, I'm thinking that we'll convert into office spaces and have onsite living suites as well." Big Eaze wanted to comfort Rose in her wanting to be close to her girls.

Rose said, "That sounds right with me, Frank. Thank you so much for thinking of me."

Frank gets up to hug Rose and mentioned, "Anything for you Rose, I don't want to see you unhappy."

As days pass.

Rose was feeling a lot better, knowing that Big Eaze was searching for the perfect building to purchase in Paris. She had informed Scarlet, Ruby and Bubbles of the search, which they were happy to hear the good news and couldn't wait for them all to unite again.

…. To be continued … abroad!

Author Bio

Carla Cuffee resides in Pennsylvania with her two adult children and young grandchild.

Carla has two publish books; **Rose's Story Fifty and Fabulous**, she likes to say, that her first book, would be an introduction to this fabulous down to earth family. And with her second book; **Rose Weds in Barbados**, carry's the entire family to a wedding in Barbados. As She continues writing her volume series on Rose's Story. The story line breathe life into a third book, **Building a Dynasty**. When not writing her volume series on Rose's Story: Carla fills her day with her close connection of family and friends. Her hobbies include reading, writing, and love creating her version of art as … " 🖤's It's me CC."